The
Stalker

ALSO BY PAULA BOMER

Baby and Other Stories
Nine Months
Inside Madeleine
Mystery and Mortality
Tante Eva

The Stalker

Paula Bomer

Published by Soho Press, Inc.
227 W 17th Street
New York, NY 10011
www.sohopress.com

Library of Congress Cataloging-in-Publication Data

Names: Bomer, Paula, author.
Title: The stalker / Paula Bomer.
Description: New York, NY : Soho, 2025.
Identifiers: LCCN 2024059138

ISBN 978-1-64129-626-7
eISBN 978-1-64129-627-4

Subjects: LCGFT: Thrillers (Fiction) | Novels.
Classification: LCC PS3602.O65496 S73 2025 | DDC 813/.6—dc23/
eng/20241210
LC record available at https://lccn.loc.gov/2024059138

Interior design by Janine Agro

Printed in the United States of America

10 9 8 7 6 5 4 3 2 1

EU Responsible Person (for authorities only)
eucomply OÜ
Pärnu mnt 139b-14
11317 Tallinn, Estonia
hello@eucompliancepartner.com
www.eucompliancepartner.com

*This one is for Hal,
for loving me through the worst*

With lies you may go ahead in the
world, but you can never go back.
                    —RUSSIAN PROVERB

He didn't look at you, he looked
through you.   —ANONYMOUS

When someone shows you who they are,
believe them.   —MAYA ANGELOU

The
Stalker

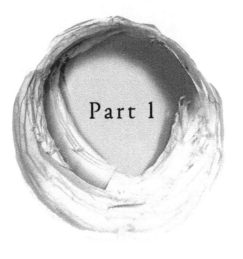

Part 1

Chapter 1

Beata was coarse. She was low-class tough, which made her masculine. She had the hair of a baby or an old woman, fine and staticky, pulled back harshly in a black rubber hair band. Her makeup was slutty, lots of black eyeliner and singed curls for bangs. She wasn't nice to the boys. No eye contact. A scowl. An air of impatience.

Doughty had a plan for her. Any of the three boys at the table would have gladly fucked her. But Beata was out of reach for Stanny and Lew. Not because she was above them. She was, clearly, beneath them. But because fucking Beata required a *plan*, some thought, some energy, maybe a bit of cunning. Doughty had this ability. His friends did not.

Beata, with her name tag above one of her tiny breasts, stood by the counter, fiddled with her stiff hair, looked into her compact, applying greasy purple-pink stuff to her lips. They had driven from Darien to Watertown, a small town with a diner and a hardware store that also sold cigarettes and potato chips. They did this to feel adventurous, to be in another world, a lowly world, a world of people with shitty jobs and cheap clothes. Darien girls would never be seen looking at themselves in a compact in public, they only did that in private. Doughty watched her smooth her apron and lick her teeth. It all happened in slow motion due to the weed they'd smoked, and in that way it felt profoundly intimate. She hated them, this he knew, so did Stanny. He was pretty sure Lew didn't know. Lew was thick.

Lew was the biggest of the three, well over six feet, and because he had grown so fast his body had parts that were larger and parts that were smaller. He was a poorly-arranged-looking guy.

Beata walked over, check pad in hand. "What can I getcha?"

"I'll have pancakes," Doughty said. He made eye contact, but only briefly. Her eyes were hard. She was tapping her pen on the pad. A tick. Impatience. She also wore, as she always did, so he noted, a small cheap-looking necklace with a glittering red heart at its center. Doughty focused on it, where it lay on her throat. A gold-colored chain, and rhinestones. Fake jewels.

"Milkshake for me," Lew said.

"Chocolate?" she scribbled.

"Yeah," he said.

"Give me a Coke," said Stanny.

She wrote it on her pad and walked away without looking up at them.

AFTER THEY FINISHED and paid, leaving pennies and a nickel for a tip, they walked back to the tree-lined path that led out of crappy, low-class Watertown up to the ivied brick buildings sprawling majestically above it. Stan had spent a summer at a cross-country camp at Taft. He told them for the millionth time that the boarding school was equipped with its own golf course, hockey rink, and pond. They sat on some rocks and smoked a joint in the privacy of the trees where the students partied at night, the ground around them littered with bottles and cans. Then they went back to Doughty's mother's station wagon and drove the hour back to Darien from Watertown.

WHEN DOUGHTY GOT home, his mother was already drunk. She was sitting in her favorite chair in the den, watching *Wheel of Fortune*. He had taken off his shoes and padded through the dining room, whose table held a scattered pile of unpaid bills, then through the never-used living room, and into the den. He sat next to her on the small couch, one his mother liked to call a "settee." His high was wearing off. She sipped her brown stuff on ice. He could smell it. Her eyes were swimming.

"How was school," she asked, trying not to slur. It was funny. She would talk slowly and try to control the movements of her mouth.

"'The Road Not Taken,'" Doughty said. Then the contestant said it.

"Bobby!" She leaned her head back and laughed. He could see the scalp under her hair. It looked red, irritated. "You're a genius!"

"Let me get us some sandwiches."

"Wonderful, Bobby," she said. "Will you get me another drink?"

He took her glass into the kitchen.

They ate cold tuna fish sandwiches in front of *Wheel of Fortune*. He focused on the winning. He liked winning. He loathed losing. It wasn't something he could accept at all, so he didn't.

"It's teen week, Bobby."

"Mom, call me Rob."

"Oh, Bobby. Don't ask me to change. I'm too old to change. Anyway, you should be on this show. You're smart enough." It was something she had said so often it had lost its meaning.

The third round was a "phrase." Six words. A seven-letter word, then a four-letter word, then three- and two- and three-letter words—small connecting words, words like "and" and "but"—then ending with a six-letter word.

"Working Your Way up the Ladder," he said. Then a contestant said it. Then everyone on the TV got excited and so did his mother. She clapped for her son.

"You got it before he did!"

"I always do, Mom."

"We have to get you on that show!"

"Yeah, Mom. And then we'll go to Tahiti."

This made her laugh. He took their plates to the kitchen. She had eaten half her sandwich. That was better than none. He dropped them in the sink, but didn't wash up. Hopefully she would before his father came home.

"I'm going out," he yelled.

"Bobby, you don't yell across the house." She said it

somewhat quietly, but he could hear her. He could hear a pin drop in the other room. It was as if he were born blind, his hearing was so acute. A house of whispering and lots of silence and some screaming does that. Yet his eyes saw everything, too. He had better than twenty-twenty vision, a rarity his pediatrician had marveled at. He closed the door to the house and got in his mother's car and started the engine and drove.

IN WATERTOWN, THE light was fading. Soon it would be dark. It was April. So close to the end of the school year, making every day seem like an eternity. But what was real and what wasn't? A day was twenty-four hours, a week was seven days. The months varied slightly. But time was just time. How it felt didn't matter.

He parked on Main Street, rolled the window all the way down, and lit a cigarette. The diner was closed, but the gate hadn't been pulled down. You could see inside the windows. From where he smoked, it was just two windows, leading into darkness. He knew it wasn't empty. Beata was in there, counting her tips, the old lady sitting down with her. There were the chairs, the small bar with the stools, the humming refrigerator. The cheap, dirty vinyl-tiled floor, engrained with a filth that stayed, no matter how often the old lady mopped it.

Working your way up the ladder. He had thought "climbing." Not working. Climbing. But the word count was wrong. No one worked themselves up any ladder. Anyone working was already losing. Working gets you nowhere, he thought. It gets you stuck at a desk or behind a mop, doing the same thing over and over again. It was one of the circles of hell. Climbing was at least grasping onto rocks, or better yet, the backs of other people. Climbing was primal. Even better yet was to be a rock. Rocks were unmovable. The last thing he wanted to be was a sad, working person. He saw it as a choice. He had choices. Everyone did.

Chapter 2

That Friday night, there was a party at a classmate's house, a square-necked boy named Charles, after a lacrosse game. Charles was a second-string lacrosse player, and his parents were at their home in the Bahamas. His parents were in the Bahamas or Vail for half the year. The home, like almost all of Darien's homes, was a sprawling, well-tended mansion, with a staff of four caretakers. Doughty had been there before. It had six bedrooms and four bathrooms, and a maid's quarter behind the kitchen.

Darien had beaten New Canaan. People were hysterical with joy. It was an hour into the party, and Stan and Lew were wasted. They had done beer bongs, then returned to the kitchen. Doughty lingered a bit longer outside where people, mostly boys, were on their knees nearly incapacitated by the tube of beer that throttled their necks as they tried to gag all that foamy liquid down. There were always a few girls there. The tomboys, the girls who wanted to compete with the men, not just the women. The aggressive girls, not quite dykes but maybe dykes, the ones who didn't even wear a little mascara, or a little lip gloss. His dick got hard watching the self-abuse, accompanied by the loud chanting and fist pumping.

In the kitchen was the land of Jell-O shots and giggling females. Jell-O shots had none of the glamour gore of beer bongs. But that was where the normal girls hung out, so of course it was a place of much excitement for his friends. No one had to prove anything, because Jell-O shots were easy and effective. It was just bam, one after another. By the time he joined Stan and Lew in the kitchen, it was clear they had done many Jell-O shots. It was funny, watching them try to talk to the girls. But boring as well.

One of the few problems of not drinking was that his dick remained very hard and undistracted and untamed by buckets of alcohol. Doughty meandered around the large house and found a bathroom in the front hallway, but then ventured further and found another, more private bathroom. He wasn't feeling adventurous enough to venture to the bathroom off the parents' bedroom, so this one would do.

The first thing anyone with half a brain did when entering a bathroom was open the cabinets and look for drugs and anything else fun, like a condom or a nice razor. He locked the door. He found some aspirin and some prescription codeine cough medicine. He took the latter. After pocketing the bottle, he saw a towel hanging on the shower rod. It was slightly damp. His dick sprang harder at the feel of that. He sniffed it. He then pulled out his cock and masturbated, looking at himself in the mirror, his handsome jawline, his wide-set blue eyes surrounded by the blond waves of his hair, smelling the towel, feeling its dampness. Getting up on his toes, he came in the sink, gripping the towel as he did.

When he returned, refreshed and relaxed, Stan and Lew were sitting side by side on a couch in the living room. Doughty sat on a large pale-green damask armchair next to them. It was a heavy chair, but he scooted it closer to his friends. Lew's hairy forearm was resting on the arm of the couch. Doughty had smooth skin, which was irksome, but it was what it was. Lew was as hairy as a Jew. Sometimes, this being one of those sometimes, he and Stan called him Jew instead of Lew, to make fun of his hairiness. Both of his friends were blacked out, so it was all fair game now. Someone was puking in the hallway bathroom. There wasn't much time left before the police came.

Doughty lit a cigarette. Flicked the flame of his lighter on, flicked it off. On and off. Then he ashed his cigarette on Lew's left arm.

"Hey, Jew, if I ash in your arm hair, it won't fall on the couch. It's like an ash trap, the greasy Jew hairs making the ash cling to it." Then Doughty ashed on Lew's neck. Lew opened his mouth to protest. Quickly, Doughty put the cherry of his cigarette on his friend's tongue. It sizzled.

Lew gagged. He even managed to jerk his head back. Quite the feat, because his neck was barely able to hold his head up. Amazing what a shot of adrenaline could do.

"What the fuck," Lew said, but it sounded like "Wha a fwa." And then he leaned forward between his shoes and threw up a stream of foamy red and yellow on the lovely carpet that was probably from Afghanistan.

This brought Stan to attention. Stan, in comparison to Lew, was so average, he wasn't as fun to play with. He wasn't loud, like Lew, and he had mousy hair and pale brown eyes. A normal face. Harder to pick on. But watching him sit up straight and show some emotion was still gratifying.

Doughty stood and grabbed Stan by the neck with both hands in a choke hold, lifting him onto his feet, then dropping him back to the couch. "Time to go, Stan the Man."

"Fucking Doughty!" Stan touched his neck. It was beet red where Doughty's hands had been. He gagged, his mouth wide and his tongue out.

Doughty heard the police sirens before anyone else. He heard them from so far away that it felt like magic, like he could hear a universe that no one else could hear.

He opened his mouth and when he was loud, when he needed to be heard, his voice came from a special place he didn't really understand, but it came, and he directed it inside Stan's ear. "LET'S GO, ASSHOLES!" Then, with the heel of his hand he whacked each one on the head. "The police are coming."

In the car, after the fresh air, the running to the vehicle, his friends were far more alert. He dropped them off at their respective driveways, and headed home.

Chapter 3

The next morning, Doughty slept well past noon. He stroked himself, listening to the lawn mower. When he heard it sputter and die, he got up. He shuffled down the hall to his bathroom, smacking his dick around until it softened, then peed. From the small window that no longer had a curtain, just an empty rusted rod, he looked out onto the lawn. His father was wrestling with the mower, pushing it back into the shed on the far reach of the lawn, next to a long line of bushes that needed trimming, a cigarette in his mouth. He appeared to be mumbling to himself, which he probably was. It was something he did in between silence and yelling. Doughty loved his father very much.

His bedroom was down a hallway that led to the kitchen, a kitchen that hadn't been updated much since it had originally served as a place where the staff cooked. It was small, a galley kitchen, with ancient appliances and a table shoved into a corner that accommodated two blue hard-backed chairs. His mother was in one, smoking.

"Bobby, you're up!" There she was in her turquoise pilled-polyester dressing gown with snaps down the middle. He was fairly certain it had been her mother's. She was happy to see him. She was probably on her third vodka with a splash of orange juice.

"Hey, Mom." He opened the fridge. There was half a loaf of bread, a half-eaten can of tuna, milk, some eggs, and an open box of Cap'n Crunch. He grabbed the cereal, sitting next to his mother at the tiny table. Her eyes were in that calm, lovely state. She was not yet swimming, but not panicking from withdrawal. This was her sweet spot. Two drinks down, just holding the third happily.

"Did you have fun last night?" she asked.

"I did, Mom." He ate a handful of cereal from the box.

"Let me get you a bowl and a spoon. Really, Bobby. I taught you manners, for heaven's sake." She stood up and opened the silverware drawer.

"Mom, I hate milk, remember?" He shoved another handful of cereal in his mouth, watching her move around, going through the motions of things she'd once done that no longer mattered. Something inside him softened momentarily. He didn't love his mother, but sometimes he felt something akin to "What a sad, old mouse she is." He guessed it was pity. A sad, old mouse, waiting for the trap to close.

"I'm going out soon." He stood, put the cereal in the fridge. They were so close he could smell her, and to Doughty's relief, she smelled good. She often did on Saturdays. She'd had a shower and she smelled like lilac perfume. The smell gave him a sharp, surgical pain in his head. A quick, thin metal spike straight to the side of his head. In and out, then gone. And yet it was his childhood, this smell. He breathed out of his mouth. Then he went and took a long shower, thinking happily about the night before, the sizzle of Lew's tongue. The feel of Stan's neck under his fingers. The tomboys painfully choking on beer bongs. He masturbated. And then he masturbated again.

On his way out, he passed his father standing half bent over a pile of junk on a table in the garage.

"Doughty!" his father yelled. "Get in here and help me!"

His father appeared to be wrestling with something inside a large toolbox. It sat open on the spider-webbed table containing a wildly disorganized plethora of rusted metal objects: shears, drills, and the like. He had two screwdrivers in his hands.

"Which one do I need for fixing the door on the shed?"

Doughty grabbed one. He had no idea what screwdriver his father needed. "You need this one."

His father was breathless, red-faced. He was probably on his way to the toilet with the screwdriver in hand, where he would spend quite some time.

"Thanks, son." He lit another cigarette even though one was burning down in the full ashtray on the table.

Doughty gave him a manly slap on the back. "No problem, Dad."

"Where you headed?"

"Over to Lew's."

His dad grunted and started out of the garage, heading to the house, in obvious discomfort.

Doughty grunted back. His father, who often exclaimed "I'm king of the castle!" when bossing his mother around. He had given Doughty so much. Not just the grunt. He knew authority mattered more than anything.

As he got in the car, he saw a bright-orange-breasted bird, a robin, land on a branch in the big oak tree in the front yard, the one tree that was probably not dead. He had learned that even after a trees dies, it produces leaves. This tree, where the bird drew his eyes, had full, solidly green leaves unlike the other four left, the other four they hadn't cut down yet, because they didn't have the money to do so. Those had pale green buds. He knew they were dead. He remembered that from the tree guy who cut a dead one down three years ago. The tree guy had said, "It's dead."

His father had been in the bathroom. Doughty was fourteen. He said, "But it has leaves."

"Those little pale things don't mean anything." The man reached out to the tree. It was one he'd climbed often as child. From it, he could look into the top windows of his house. The three windows that faced that tree were his parents' bedroom, the small window of his parents' bathroom, and his own room. Up high in that tree, he saw everything and no one saw him and it felt right.

The man easily pulled some bark off the tree. "See how brittle it is?" He passed it to Doughty.

Doughty rubbed it between his fingers and it crumbled. Then the man reached up to a low, thin branch and cracked a twig.

"See this?" he said, showing the small, circular barrel of the twig to Doughty. "It's brown. If the veins were green, then it would be alive. It's brown and dry—it's dead."

"So the leaves are fake," he said.

The man laughed. "Yes, the leaves are just a sad attempt to look alive."

Then they both laughed.

Then the man said, "Just not giving up! Stupid tree."

Doughty smiled. He remembered thinking the tree was smart, but he said nothing.

THE MERRITT PARKWAY was a beautiful road, this was certain. It wound through Fairfield County, lulling back and forth, each covered bridge unique, enveloped by beautiful trees, all very much alive, a forest protected by law. A small, well-kept road, narrow and curving, known for its own signage, its own quiet, exclusive beauty, its own everything. No trucks could get under the bridges, no buses from the city. This was Moses's plan, the man who'd designed it, to keep out the riffraff. To keep out Black people. It worked. It was about ownership, about exclusivity. Just driving through it, turning the wheel gently to the left then to the right, caused a sort of hypnotism. He leaned into the curves, his head slightly leaning, too. His father's family had been in this part of Connecticut since before Merritt was built by Moses, before it opened in 1940. His father's family knew Moses. His grandfather had gone to Yale with him. His father repeated this often, and it had annoyed him for a small time, really only during the onset of puberty, when Doughty briefly had been rebellious against his old man and his old-man ways.

This was before he realized that knowing where he was from, knowing his heritage, meant everything. Knowing his place in the world meant knowing his due, meant knowing who he was. When he turned off the Merritt, he took the small back roads to Watertown.

It was 4:50 P.M. From where he was parked he could see the kitchen guy come out, lugging two large garbage bags to the dumpsters behind the diner. A cloud passed over the sun. With his window down, he heard the creak and thud of the dumpster lids.

Then Beata walked out with the older woman. Beata pulled the gate down. He heard the old lady say, "See you, darlin'," and watched her pat Beata on the shoulder. Beata started taking off her apron. It was double tied around her small waist into a bow in the front. He heard her exhale. A sigh of relief. Absentmindedly, she rolled her apron into a small, tight ball, looking off into the street. He got out of his car, crossed the street, and quickly walked toward her.

Beata. She was a bird. Not only in the old-fashioned sense of using it as a term for a woman, but in that she looked like a bird. Her face was sharp, a face made for pecking hopelessly, looking around quickly without settling on anything for long. Furtive. Fearful. About to take flight. Her pointy shoulders exposed, she wore a tight, cheap-looking red tank top and acid-washed jeans, also tight, her hip bones jutting out.

"Hi, Beata," he said. He had startled her.

"Oh! Hi?" She held her black fake-leather purse tightly against her hip. It was still light out, a yellowing late-afternoon sky.

"You know me. I come in with my friends." He smiled, closed mouth, hiding his chipped tooth. He rarely thought about his chipped tooth, but he instinctively covered it with his thick lips when he smiled.

He could see himself in Beata's eyes. His bright blond hair fashionably shaggy, his loose angelic curls touching his neck.

"Oh, yeah, hi." She did her bird thing. Looking around furtively. "Where are they?"

He had a tiny pang of concern that she liked Lew. Thick, dark-haired, hairy Lew. It couldn't be Stanny. "I came here to see *you*." And it worked. She stopped pecking around for a minute, her gaze on him. She was flattered.

"Oh." She smiled, looked down.

He watched her shoulders relax, but then—the birdlike thing of flight started up again and she started swinging her bag around.

"Want to smoke in Midway? I also have beers in the car." He nodded over to his car. She looked at it like she was weighing things. Finally she said that her mom was expecting her home for dinner.

"Where's home?"

"Waterbury. My dad's cousin owns this diner. I take the five thirty-two bus. Usually."

"What part of Waterbury?"

"The South End."

"Let's have a beer and a smoke. Then I'll drive you back to Waterbury."

"How do you have a car? I thought you guys weren't allowed to have a car?"

Of course, she thought they were from Taft. "I live in Darien. I don't go to Taft."

"Oh." Her face softened. Her mouth actually was a wide one, even if her lips were thin. "That's far."

"I like to drive." She had barely looked him in the eye, but she did for a second. Her pale blue eyes, sunken in dark eye sockets. "It relaxes me. Driving."

"Can you get me home by seven?"

"Sure. Let me get the beers."

They walked to his car and he got his backpack with the beers. He loved his backpack. It was large, but not too large, and it was sturdy and classy, L.L.Bean, navy of course. With inner pockets, but not too many. As they turned up Midway, he let her walk in front of him, a move to seem as if he were being polite, the "after you" thing, the idea that he was somehow protecting her in case she were to fall. It wasn't that steep, but it was uphill, and really he was looking at her ass, which was sad, narrow hipped, and flat.

Soon, they were sitting on the rocks, smoking. She had a pack of Kools. As she leaned forward toward his lighter, she kept her knees together. He gave her a tall boy of Budweiser.

"I have a joint," he said, producing one from his pack of Merits. He gauged her expression. She was nonplussed. This was good.

"Okay," she said.

He lit it, took a big hit, passed it to her.

"This is some good shit," she said, choking on the hit, holding it in like a pro. Whoosh, she exhaled.

"Right?" he said. It was. It was from a light-green, sticky

bud, with little red veins through it. He had gotten it from a classmate who had been in New York for a weekend and brought back the good shit.

Here are the issues with getting someone high. You can't get them just a little high, because if the person is just a little high, their senses become acute, that thing called "paranoia," and it can actually make them more suspicious of other people's intentions. He looked at Beata, watched the awareness come into her eyes, a sort of solemnity. "Here," he said, passing it to her. She hesitated. He held it there, raised his eyebrows, smiled. She took it and smoked. This would do it. Getting her higher.

"You have a pretty mouth," he said.

She touched her lips. "I do?" She passed it back to him. He took a drag, then passed it back to her.

"No, man. I'm good." She waved it away.

"Come on, it's Saturday." He thrust it at her. "Come on. It's such good shit."

And it was. The air was a rich perfume of it. She took another drag, looking at him warily. So she wasn't totally dumb, which was a good thing. There wasn't a man alive who didn't want a bit of a challenge.

The joint gone, they sat there high as fuck. She said something, but he wasn't listening, although he could hear her cotton mouth. She sipped her beer and took a lip gloss out of her purse, rubbing it onto her lips.

"What a pretty mouth."

She laughed gently.

He stretched his arm out and touched her lips. She pulled

back, but just a little. "Did you ever have braces?" He kept his finger on her lip.

Then she shook him off and he dropped his hand for a moment. "No."

"Let me see your teeth," he said, and quickly moved his finger back onto her mouth, pushing her upper lip toward her nose.

She shook him off again, but then, like a child at the dentist, she opened her mouth for him. Teeth gritted, chin up. She had crooked bottom teeth, like an old fence, some leaning back, some a bit sideways.

"I have a chipped tooth," he said, opening his mouth. He also was missing two molars in the back, but he didn't show her that. It was genetic, his father had said. He hadn't been to the dentist since grade school. "Dentists are thieves and liars," his father had bellowed once. Really, they didn't have the money. "I got it in a fight," he lied. He got it tripping and falling in his backyard when he was ten.

She looked at his tooth. "I'm really high," she said, and did the slow high laugh.

"Drink your beer, it'll help."

"Yeah, I know," she said. She drank. "Wow, I'm so high."

He put his hand back on her lip.

"Stop it."

"I can't help it." He was hard. "Open your mouth. You have such a wide mouth."

Confused, she opened her mouth just a bit, and he shoved two fingers in it, pushing at the roof of her mouth. She struggled away and he grabbed the back of her head until she gagged. She got up and stumbled back, but he was up now, too, holding her by her upper arms.

"Hey," she said, then he leaned in and kissed her and kissed her again.

"I'm crazy about you," he said. "I have been for a long time."

"You said you'd take me home." She was present now. She lurched out of his grip and made it a few steps before she had to hold on to a tree for balance.

"Okay, Beata, let's go."

AFTER HE DROPPED her off at her broken-ass-looking house, with her address burned in his head and finding out her last name, Murphy, of course she was part Mick, he drove off to the Merritt Parkway, and as he rocked the steering wheel left and right, the sun setting over the idyllic bridges and the very-much-alive, well-tended trees, he had a sense of calm, a sense of rightness in the world.

Chapter 4

When he got home, his mother came into the hall. She was still in her turquoise bathrobe. She was on the downside of the bell curve of drinking, tired, no longer having any fun.

"Lew called. He said for you to call him."

"Thanks, Mom."

He went into his room, where he had a small television, a VCR, and his own telephone. He dialed Lew, who picked up. He'd been hoping Lew's mother or his sister, Kristen was her name, would pick up. They both had large breasts and he enjoyed trying to charm them. Lew's mom, Heather, dressed like a grown woman, more so than many of the Darien mothers in their infantile Laura Ashley dresses and their gardening clogs. She was often in exercise clothes, having come back from an aerobics class. Just showing everything, her thick hips, the tight aerobic pants crawling up her butt crack and cupping the U-shape of her pussy. He got hard thinking of Lew's mom's pussy.

"Doughty?" Lew said, sounding like he had a marble in his mouth. "Wha the fuc id you do, you psycho? My songue is burn!"

"What? Say again?" Doughty sat down on his bed. He leaned on the pillows against the headboard, kicked off his shoes, stretched out his legs, and looked at his boner in his pants. He put the phone in the crook of his neck and crossed both his hands behind his head.

"Hanny said ew pu a cigareh en ma mou!"

"Oh, that!" Doughty said. "You guys were so drunk. You dared me to. Then you basically forced me to. You don't remember? You were really drunk."

"Fuh you, Doughty, why wou I as you to ah? Fuhin iar." He sounded like he was going to cry, but it was hard to tell because he couldn't really talk. "My ma thins I shou o to a ospita."

"First, I'm not lying. I was smoking and you grabbed my hand and put it in your mouth. Secondly, you don't need to go to the hospital. Here is the good news. Your mouth has amazing capacities to heal quickly. It heals exactly twelve times faster than any other part of your skin. It has easier access to the blood supply because the tissue is rich in blood vessels. The healing time is something like forty-nine and a half hours. So you'll be fine for school on Monday."

There was a silence. Sometimes it was hard to be the knowledgeable one. It was as if he were their teacher. His friends didn't read encyclopedias like he did. So he was constantly teaching them things.

"I know this from when I was a Boy Scout," he added.

"Fu you."

"Want to go see a movie tomorrow?"

"No."

"Let's go see *Back to the Future Part II* again!"

"Uck u."

"It'll be fun!"

Lew hung up on him. Doughty sighed and turned on the television. His father was yelling at his mother, so he turned it up. Then he heard a knock so he got up and turned the sound down and opened the door. There she stood.

"Are you coming out for dinner?"

She looked hopeful but sad. So funny, those two things together.

"Nope. I'm watching my show."

"I made a casserole."

"Put it in the fridge, Ma. I'll microwave it later."

"Okay, Bobby. You know I prefer Mom. We are not living on a farm."

"Okay, MOM! Okay, Mother," he said, making a funny face. Then he leaned into her. His face up near hers. It was like inhaling from the gas tank of her car. "*And I'm not Bobby.*"

He watched her scuffle away, then he shut and locked the door. Jumped back onto the bed. In the drawer next to him, he kept the phone book. He opened it up. It was the large one, for all of Connecticut. It was a tome. He looked up Murphy on 12½ Brendan Street, enjoying carefully turning the thin pages. There were many Murphys, but only the one on Brendan Street. Bingo. 227-4668. He said it three times out loud. Then he called.

A man picked up. He hung up. Beata. A pot of gold. That was Irish. She was a pot of cheap, fake, shitty leprechaun gold. But gold she was.

Chapter 5

After school on Monday, Doughty, Lew, and Stan went out the back entrance where everyone smoked. He felt a distance between them, but it wasn't a wall, it wasn't anything he hadn't had to deal with in the past. In fact, it was necessary to solidify his dominance over the two. Both of his friends were dressed for cross-country, in tiny nylon shorts and tank tops. He looked at Lew's hairy arms. Then Lew stroked his left arm. Ha! Like he remembered that. Maybe he'd gotten a little singed there, too?

"How's your tongue, Lewlew," Doughty said. He lit his cigarette. "Do you guys want to go to the diner?"

"Fuck you, Doughty," Lew said.

"See! I told you the mouth has so many blood vessels, it heals up to twenty-one times faster than the rest of the body," Doughty said, and gave him a gentle, but still manly, pat on his shoulder. "You're an animal when you get fucked up!"

"At least we got out before the cops came in," Stanny said. "Give me a smoke, Doughty."

Doughty handed him one and lit it for him. "And you have me to thank for that!"

They seemed not quite convinced. But it was true. He had helped them! He was always helping people. "Did anyone get arrested?"

"No," Stanny said. "Charles knew all the cops. Well, his father does. They just made everyone go home."

"Were there any crashes?"

"One girl had a fender bender in her driveway."

Doughty was disappointed. "That's not bad."

They stood in silence. This was not something remarkable, three adolescent boys standing in silence, in the small cement area not visible from the parking lot or the football field, the most private area outside the school. The outdoor equivalent to the often-empty music room, or a closed stall in the boys' bathroom. Yet Doughty occasionally liked to fill the silence. "I think I'm going to fuck the waitress."

His friends perked up.

"Doughty, you fucking dog! She's gonna give you some nasty whore disease!" Stanny said.

"Fucking put a rubber on it before sticking it in that skank," Lew added.

"I don't wear condoms. Who wears a fucking condom." He flicked his cigarette butt a good distance.

"When you fuck a nasty townie whore, you wear a condom, Doughty," Stanny said.

"So you're the one with the condom stash, huh, Stanny?"

Now they were all jostling one another. All was good again. He could smell his friends, smell their adolescent boy stink. Their raging hormonal stink.

"I don't fuck nasty townie skanks," Stanny said. "You just got that fever from your father, because your mother is white trash. Family of skank-fuckers."

Doughty grabbed him. Got right up in his face. "Watch out, Stanny. Your mother is next! You know she likes me."

Stanny struggled and then broke free. Actually, he *would* fuck Stanny's mother, too, although he liked Lew's better. Stan swung, but Doughty ducked, and Stan stumbled and almost fell.

"Bring it, Stanny!" Doughty said.

"Fucking couldn't pay me to fuck your mom," Stan said.

"Oh snap!" Lew said. Then he high-fived Stan. "Okay, Stan the Man, let's go to practice. See you later, Doughty the Degenerate. Have fun doing nothing all afternoon."

On his drive home, Doughty thought about how perfectly he'd avoided Stan's swing. He attributed this to *The Karate Kid*. *The Karate Kid* was his secret weapon. He had watched it in the den with his mother many times. It was a thing they could agree on. The first *Karate Kid*, which was the best one, had come out five years ago, followed by *Part II* and then by *Part III*, which had been released just this year. So many things had changed since the first one came out, yet so many things were the same. *The Karate Kid* was still the same. It was a source of power. He'd learned so much from it, like how to take wisdom from just about anything. Obviously, there was the shelf of encyclopedias in the living room. And the dictionary. And the thesaurus. Those were incredibly important. But he memorized certain things from *The Karate Kid*. "It's okay to lose to an opponent, but never to FEAR!" Any idea of fear was really a dull memory, a hardened thing in the back of his mind. If a flicker of it came to him, he long ago had learned to kill it. Fear was dead to him. When Mr. Miyagi asked Daniel if he was ready to learn karate, Daniel responded: "I guess so." Then Mr. Miyagi made Daniel learn not to guess. To do.

To win, there was no "guess so." Miyagi used the analogy of a road, and explained it to Daniel like this: walking on the left side of the road is fine, walking on the right side of the road is fine, but walking down the middle of the road will eventually get you "squished."

Doughty noticed people mostly walked down the middle. And even if they weren't walking down the middle, they could waver, and that was where you wanted them. That was where you could get them, start the squishing. At first he wasn't sure where he was walking, but what he knew was that he was always on the outside. He walked on the outside, whether it was on the left or the right. If he was walking down the hallway with Stanny and Lew, Doughty walked on the left. He attributed this and many things to being left-handed. He also walked behind people. This he got from another favorite movie of his, *The Godfather*. In *The Godfather*, all the bosses sat with their backs to the wall, so they could see everything. When he walked behind people, his back was essentially to the wall, he could see everything he needed to, he could monitor the people in front of him. These two movies, *The Godfather* and *The Karate Kid*, he owned on VHS and was able to watch over and over again in the privacy of his room.

One thing about *The Karate Kid* that he knew to be true from watching other movies as well, was that it was an ideal. Ideals were like clichés, in that they were true. In *The Karate Kid*, like most movies, the male is dark-haired and the female is blond. The girl is loyal, and the boy is protective, which really meant "in control." This was just how things worked. Doughty had wavy blond hair. Sometimes, mostly in the past, it enraged him. To calm himself about this, he just thought of it as something he would outgrow. People's hair darkened with age. And no one was without a weakness, and his hair was a minor one. He focused on his strengths. And even if he wasn't dark-haired, his soft, curly blond locks made people look. Life wasn't perfect. That was another true thing. It was what you did with your strengths.

When he got home, he made it to his room without seeing anyone. He put in *The Karate Kid* and lit a cigarette. Daniel's biggest problem was that he didn't realize that once he'd taken that wisdom from Miyagi, he should've gotten rid of the old man. Daniel had beaten the stupid jocks, gotten the girl. Now he needed to totally get rid of the old Asian loser. It was important to squish people when you were done with them. Daniel didn't understand that after you get what you need, you move on to get more of what you need. You can't get everything from one person. People are to be fed off of. This he got all by himself. But *The Karate Kid* had helped a lot.

His mother had bought him the tie-in book, too. He

watched the movie more than he looked at the book. Yet he kept the book under his bed in a toolbox, with his other important stuff. It was the same toolbox his father had in the shed, the one filled with the tools his father would never learn how to use. His father had gotten him the matching one for his twelfth birthday. He had said, "Son, you're old enough to have your own toolbox." Within a few months, his father had forgotten all about it, and Doughty had moved it under his bed, using it to store the cigarettes he stole from them. That was another thing: when you get something, you use it for what you need, which wasn't always what it was originally meant for. But mostly, squishing is important. Daniel needed to squish Miyagi after he got all he needed from him. It was possible the people who wrote the movies weren't smart enough to understand that. It was something he knew, and it wasn't something he shared. To have power one must have secrets. This, too, he had figured out. To withhold knowledge is to keep power.

Squish. He looked that up in the dictionary. The word "squish" dated back to the mid-seventeenth century. It meant "to make a soft squelching sound when walked on or in." Or, even better, "to yield or cause to yield easily to pressure; squash." Here were the synonyms: Flatten. Pound. How easy it would be to flatten an old person. Pound pound until the old person was flat.

He lit another cigarette as the movie played. At one point, he tried to keep count of how many times he'd watched it, but then he decided it wasn't necessary. Miyagi was explaining that there's a specific order of things in karate just like in nature. He also explained how defense is the best offense. That once you move away and let the other person fall, then you can really go in for the kill. When you have someone down, then you can dominate. But first comes the fall. It was sort of like God. That was another interesting book on the shelf, the Bible. He didn't miss church, which he'd stopped attending with his mother at the age of twelve, but he still had a thing for the Bible. In particular, there was the version of the Bible for school-age children that was way more like looking things up in the dictionary, nice and straightforward. It cut to the chase. The main idea was that after man falls, he is ashamed. And once someone is ashamed, then you really have them. Then you have the power.

Chapter 6

On Thursday after school, he drove to the diner. Beata worked Monday, Thursday, and Saturday. He chose a different spot today, just to liven things up, one block farther away from the diner. He could hear the gate come down. Then he saw her exit the building with the old lady, watched them say their goodbyes. Soon, he was behind her.

"Hi, Beata."

He'd startled her. "Oh hey, Doughty." The surprise turned quickly to calm. That bothered him. But he shook it off, remembering his fingers hard in her mouth. He smiled, stood up straighter. One of the problems with Beata was that she was tall. He stood up even straighter.

"Do you want a ride home?"

"Sure," she said.

"Let's go." He put a hand on her arm. "Do you want to get high?"

"No, I can't. I have homework."

In the car, he lit her Kool. She was wearing an orange-and-green-striped T-shirt. Her mascara was clumpy. But, her mouth. He exhaled smoke out the window, looking away. He was hard. He shoved his fist into his dick. It helped. It was a perfect spring day. The breeze was just right, blowing his locks around his head, his arm resting out the window. They were quiet for most of the ride.

"What's your favorite subject?" Doughty asked.

"Health. I want to be a nurse," she said. "Not gonna lie, I like that they show a lot of videos in health." She smiled at him, her thin lips stretching out even thinner, her teeth impressively white.

"It's an easy class."

"I have my own VCR in my room."

"Wow. Cool."

"Here," she said, "right here." He drove another block. "Wait, you passed it."

He parked. "Can I come in and meet your parents?"

"They're not home from work yet. My mom works the night shift tonight and my stepfather is probably still at the garage."

BEATA, HIS BIRD. His father used to refer to women as "birds." Birds had amazing brains, even though their brains were small. And regardless of their brains, they were something to be caught. And put in a cage.

Her head turned toward the window as she opened the door. He examined her profile. She could peck away with that face. And her neck! Twisting back and forth, facing him when she had something to say, facing away to blow smoke. It was a bird neck, moving that head to look around quickly, nervously. Mobile. Some birds could twist their heads all the way around. Well, owls. She was no owl. What kind of bird was she? She didn't have the ferocity of a blue jay. Maybe she was a robin. The bird that no one gave a shit about.

As they walked toward her house, Doughty exclaimed, "So we have the place to ourselves!"

"My younger brother will be home."

"How old is he?"

"Ten."

"I would love a glass of water or something. And to use your bathroom if that's okay."

"Sure."

He walked up the rickety wooden steps behind her, up to a sad porch with two flimsy plastic chairs and a matching plastic table with a full ashtray on it. It was a narrow, two-story house, about twenty feet wide, neighbors around twelve feet on either side of the house. He watched her use the key. It was a key-in-knob lock, the kind you just needed a credit card to open. He saw that the doorjamb was loose. When they got in, she had to slam the door to get the nearly busted lock to cinch.

And there they were, in her home. She wiped her feet on the welcome rug, then he did the same. It was important to demonstrate moments of respect even if it was just for show. She was naive enough *not* to be ashamed of her house, but she wasn't stupid enough not to know where and what Darien was. Maybe she didn't care? That would be interesting, a tough-to-impress type. But he could manage that. He could make her see her position in the world in comparison to his own. Kings of castles know how to do that. And surely she already had some idea.

Her house was, in every way, a sad, poor person's house. He was a little taken aback about how unfazed she was. Even in Waterbury, there must be nicer neighborhoods to which she could compare herself. He wasn't feeling her shame, or even something close. Was it something like modesty? She just exuded this straightforwardness that was unnerving, but only slightly. He was a Savile. She was a waitress. A plebe.

As they walked through the living room, with its floor carpeted in dark beige shag, her younger brother, sporting a mullet, came in, insulted her, then disappeared up the stairs, which were also carpeted in the same awful shag. It was not the right carpet for stairs, didn't they know that? There was a smell, too. Then he saw it. The cause of the smell. A dying old mutt sat on the plaid couch and wagged its tail pathetically. She said, "Hi, Benji," patted it, then went into the kitchen.

He took a seat at the table. The yellow vinyl floors and green fern wallpaper were deeply tragic in their desire to be cheerful.

"Do you want something to drink?" She opened the fridge, and he saw the cheap cartons of milk and juice, six-packs of Diet Coke stacked on top of each other, no-brand eggs, and no-brand white bread. No Pepsi, his favorite. Four TV dinners were on a shelf. Why were TV dinners in the fridge? It was utterly bizarre. He debated telling Beata that they should be stored in the freezer. She looked at Doughty and her face hardened.

"Want a Diet Coke?"

"Sure," he said. Then he nodded toward the staircase and said, "Show me your house."

She peeled off two cans. He cracked his open and followed her tiny ass, the ass of a little boy, the kind of ass he'd had at eleven, up the stairs to the second floor. On the landing there were three doors. He could hear her brother listening to the AM radio in one room. The brother came out and yelled something, and Beata pushed him back into his room and slammed his door shut.

"This is my room," she said, and opened her door, right next to the brother's. He looked in briefly but decided he needed to see the bathroom first.

"Where's the bathroom?"

"It's downstairs. Down the hall toward the back of the house. I'll take you." Like a good soldier, she led the way back down and pointed him down a dark hallway.

He entered. He picked up a shining, clean, half-empty bottle of perfume sitting next to the bathroom sink. Charlie, he'd seen the ads. Why were the poor always so tidy, dusting their fucking perfume bottles? He opened the cabinet. A bottle of aspirin, cheap lipsticks, and face makeup, some Ivory soap bars, and a few prescriptions. The only one of interest was a muscle relaxant his father had. He opened it, saw there were only two pills in it, and decided against it. When he unzipped his fly his dick stood up at him, and he slapped it a few times so he could take a piss.

He left, closed the door behind him, and briefly opened the basement door to look down a green, smelly cement staircase, then returned to Beata.

"Let's go back up," he said.

—

AND THERE THEY were. A twin bed with a pink polyester bedspread, dolls and teddy bears propped up on pillows that were encased with various frilly, machine-embroidered cases with sayings on them. One said "live, laugh, love."

"When does your stepdad get back?"

She had sat on the bed. "At seven or eight, or later, depending if he goes out for a drink."

He walked back to the door and latched it shut. Turning back to face the room, he saw there was one window that looked out on the small alley between her house and the next house, but there was a gauzy curtain covering the view.

He walked up to her and touched her face. She moved it ever so slightly.

"Are you a virgin?" he asked.

"Yeah."

He sat next to her on the bed and kissed her gently. Her eyes were closed. He pulled back so slightly, a flutter away, and when he did this, her mouth would open wider, confused, and come closer to his. Then he would stay as still as a fox, and then he'd push forward a bit, and pull back and forth, and on it went.

She moaned, so he dabbed his tongue into her open mouth, then onto her lips, a hand on her cheek. He put his other hand on her padded bra and she let him, so he sat back and quickly took off his shirt and then hers, but she wouldn't take off her bra, the shame of it being stuffed was his guess, so he moved to her zipper. She pushed him back a little, then stood and took off her pants herself, standing in her underwear. He took off his pants and then his underwear and his dick sprang out at her. She looked at it. Then she got on her knees and took it into her mouth.

This was a surprise.

"Where'd you learn that?"

She took it out for a moment, leaning her head back to talk. "My cousin."

Then she went at it. It didn't take long, and she swallowed and stood up.

She was breathing a little heavy, wiping her mouth, and he carefully laid her back on her bed and she put her arms over her head while he took off her underwear. She had a few fine, long, dark hairs on her pussy and he got hard again and tried to jam it in her. It wasn't really working, so he stopped and went down on her.

She sat up and pulled away. "What are you doing?"

So her cousin hadn't taught her this. "Relax," he said.

"No," she said.

"Come on, lie back."

"No way."

He wanted to eat her pussy some more, so he ignored her, and as he did, she got so wet and started making noises and she pulled away, which made his dick insane. He sat up, spat on his hand, gave his dick a quick lubing, and stuck it in, eventually finding some room. Jesus it was tight and she was biting her hand, all red-faced. He stopped looking at her face and got to work. It wasn't easy. But it was quick. And then it was done. He rolled off her and looked at the blood on his dick.

"You all right?"

She looked at the wall. "Yeah."

———

WHEN SHE WALKED him to the door, her brother came running after them. "I'm going to tell! I'm going to tell!"

She went to smack him, her hand pulled back, and he ran back up the stairs laughing. At the door he kissed her and her eyes softened and he knew it, he was in. He was in and he had to keep digging. He'd found a little gold mine, nah, a nickel mine, a dirt hole in a backyard that would never hit rock. A bottomless pit. All his. His Irish fake gold.

As he started the car he thought, What a day! The thing was, once you took someone's virginity, you became special. He knew he was special but the important thing was that now *she knew* he was special, and now he had her in his pocket. He'd stolen her virginity. She'd given herself to him. He was her first. She was his now. *She would never forget him, her first.* He had marked her. Every day, even the little wins count. Mr. Miyagi would agree. He would tell Stan and Lew. Not sure when and how, but once he was calmer, he'd figure out a way.

Part 2

Chapter 7

Doughty's father died over Christmas break Doughty's junior year at Boston College. He met with an estate lawyer, who informed him that his mother wasn't in the will, nor was his mother's name on the house. Doughty was the sole benefactor. He knew his father had done that to keep the money in the Savile family. He appreciated his father for that. His father was a smart man, a man of good breeding.

"There is debt. A lot of debt. Essentially, the bank owns the house. There are three hundred and forty-five dollars in a checking account that your father has left over from his disability payments, which effectively are now over."

"How do I get the three hundred forty-five dollars?" Doughty asked. "And my name is on the house? So I own it?"

"Technically, yes," the lawyer said.

"I'm a homeowner! I've always been interested in real estate. This is great news."

"Robert, I don't think I'm getting through to you on this, so call the bank and set up a meeting."

—

THE NEXT DAY, Doughty visited the bank. "So I own the house now?"

"Well, no. The bank has owned it for some time. There is about five hundred thousand dollars of debt. Your father had a reverse mortgage."

"The house is worth half a million dollars?" Doughty was impressed, but not that impressed. He was, after all, a Savile. A Darien man.

"We would need to do an inspection and so on, but the bank can probably get half that if we are lucky when we go into foreclosure. The bank would handle it and take any losses. You just need to sign this. Otherwise, you inherit the debt."

"So, I could make a quarter million dollars?" This was such good news.

The bank man looked at him but Doughty focused on one of the photos on the desk. It was of the bank man and his family. People and their photos of their families. What garbage. But it was there to look at, so he did. Out of his side-eye, he saw the man get up.

"I think you need to come back another time. Maybe bring your mother? Robert?"

The man walked to the door and opened it. Doughty was fairly comfortable. He was thinking about what he could do with a quarter million dollars, thinking how he probably wouldn't be stuck in some bank office in Darien. No, not him.

"Robert, I have to ask you to leave. I have another

appointment. But you really should sign off on this. You do not want to be saddled with a half a million in debt."

HIS MOTHER WAS drinking even more. Was she celebrating? She was probably afraid. She was always afraid and always celebrating. She had taken some shit job at a flower shop in town run by her church friend, Mrs. Hutton, who also rented her the apartment above the shop where he was crashing while taking care of his inheritance. The job gave her health insurance, so her occasional hospital visits from her drinking were basically covered. This was pretty much all he knew.

While his father was dying, he'd gotten some sympathy from Stanny and Lew. He hadn't been in touch with them that much since they went off to college. He knew this was typical of young men and he didn't take it personally. His ability not to take things personally was a great asset. He had held his father's hand out of duty and watched the old man croak. It was a long and boring process, yet looking back, he wished it had taken longer, because there could have been more sympathy. His mother had been at work when his father croaked. Doughty looked up "croak" in the dictionary: "(of a frog or crow) to make a characteristic deep hoarse sound. 'The frogs settled in the shade, croaking happily.'" It was quite right, the word "croak." And while watching his father die, listening to the rattling of breath, the animal noises, and that thing, like even a fly does, where the body tried not to die, he also thought about the visuals, not just the noise. He thought of a frog, neck pushed forward, throat struggling upward. He saw and heard the death thing and saw the sad dying struggle, the trying not to die. It was fascinating. It was why boys captured bugs in jars and watched them die. Or shot deer. Or strung up a cat.

After his father croaked, he'd packed all the encyclopedias, the dictionary, the thesaurus, his VHS tapes, his toolbox, everything that mattered, and had gone to his mother's apartment and dumped them there. The couch in her new apartment sucked, but he felt surrounded by all this knowledge. It was temporary, so he actually slept well. He was able to withdraw the $345 and close his father's account. He was loaded! That, he kept a secret. Life was good.

During that time, the mystique of his father dying made him glow. No one else's father had died. The attention was great. A mother of a classmate he vaguely knew came up to him, putting her fat, ring-laden hand on his shoulder, and said, "My deepest condolences." He produced a tear for her. There had been three casseroles given to them by neighbors, which were pretty good, especially the one with pasta and a shit ton of cheese. Knowing his father was dying, all his teachers passed him right before the holidays started without him doing any work. It was such a great time. He had seen Lew and Stanny once in town and they had exchanged numbers. He noticed some reluctance in their eyes, but it wasn't severe. He thought he could relax, hang out, while his mystique grew, but shortly after the lawyer told him everything, he chose to take the Greyhound bus back to Boston. It was good to take a break from his mother's apartment, from dealing with the duties of handling the Savile estate. The spring semester was starting. He often missed classes, and upon his return, he stopped going altogether, although he didn't inform anyone. Unlike his fellow students, he was ready to move on. School was for children. He was a man now.

He lived in Lower Allston with Moses, a Mexican man who was his coworker. Doughty bused tables part-time with him at a tourist restaurant that sold clams in Faneuil Hall. Moses was also a small-time coke dealer. Doughty had a girlfriend, also a student at Boston College, Stephanie Erwin from Pennsylvania. He usually stayed at her apartment in the Back Bay, even though he wasn't crazy about her roommate, or roommates. He was never quite sure if she had one or two of them. There often were other women around, which was annoying, but nothing he couldn't handle. It was a comfortable apartment, overlooking Commonwealth Avenue.

Stephanie was from Bryn Mawr, a part of Pennsylvania known as "mainline Philadelphia," and although the people from there were always wealthy and usually had some historical connection to old money, it was still Pennsylvania, and New England families like his own had the obligation and the joy, let's face it, to look down upon them. He had the duty to put Stephanie in her place. She had undoubtedly learned to accept her place in the social ladder when she went to boarding school. She had gone to Millbrook School, a particularly small place known for having its own zoo that consisted of a sad black bear and some large bird that couldn't fly anymore. Mostly, it was known for accepting dumb, rich girls like Stephanie.

Like most dumb girls, she was studying psychology. When he hung out with other dudes at BC, they loved to make fun of the dumb girls who studied psychology. All of his male friends were studying business. Despite some of his friends giving him shit for fucking someone beneath him, fucking anyone regularly was quite the feat at college. And he'd fucked her a lot. For over a year now.

He often leafed through her textbooks, scoffing at her stupidity. She seemed mostly to care about her wardrobe and her social life, about who would get engaged and who would not, and somewhere in the back of her thick head, he knew that she understood that they would never marry. He was too good for her.

He enjoyed aspects of her, despite her questionable social status and being thick. She literally had a thick head, too; she wasn't just mentally thick. She had a particularly big head, one he would roll around in his hands sometimes. It weighed as much as a bowling ball. But that was okay because her tits were even larger than her head.

There was something so satisfying about a girl with tits larger than her head, each one a softer, and more fun, larger head. Two larger heads that were tits instead of heads. As dumb as she was, she knew her tits were amazingly huge. Understandably, she was proud of them. There were many things he could do with her tits that were fun.

First, and most importantly, there was parading her around in front of other boys. The male species knows big tits regardless. Like any girl with huge tits, even if they try to hide them, there they were, on display despite baggy sweaters, or crossed arms; the mound of boobs was there. This was great currency among men, having a girl with huge tits to show off, as meaningful as a really nice car, or a Rolex.

When he first got Stephanie out of her shirt and bra, there was a disappointment, nearing disgust. The huge tits dropped to her waist and swayed off to the sides of her body and were riddled with stretch marks and punctuated with plate-size nipple areas. Once he got over that, he got the hang of them, and they were fun. They were like extra butt cheeks. You could fuck them with your dick. You could put your face in between them, you could mash them about—eventually turn the mashing into smacking and then smack harder and harder, depending on the girl—and what else? They were tits. They were endless fun. Oh, you could come all over them. That was something, although he preferred her face, though for some reason she was opposed to it. He did it once in a while anyway, pretending it was an accident.

When she broke up with him, he knew it was coming. She had shown a lot of sympathy about his father dying but after a few months of taking care of him and cooking for him and spending money on him, scrambling eggs for him and making his toast how he liked it, not too crunchy because of his teeth, always picking up the bill when they went out to the Vietnamese place, and even giving him money when he didn't have any, which was all the time, she sort of stopped being nice. He didn't give up easily. Why get rid of a cow if it still produces milk? Wasn't that a saying? She had more in her to give. It wasn't his teeth that were bothering her. The vast majority of rich kids' parents pretended they didn't have any money and many of their children had bad teeth. Dentists were seen as a waste of the money that they pretended they didn't have. In his case, there really wasn't any money at all, and this was something he'd correct soon enough, once he wrapped his head around it, made the time to take care of his family fortune. So outwardly, he was just like all the other extraordinarily well-off students. Bad teeth. Shabby clothes. His currency, like the rest of his social class, was his class itself. His *ancestry*. Despite his having excellent ancestry, he borrowed stuff sometimes. On a rare moment when Doughty was walking with Stephanie through the Commons, he pointed to a statue.

"That's my great-uncle." He had noticed the statue had his last name spelled differently. The statue was of a Harold Seville Spencer.

"Really?" she said, trying to hold his hand. He had a rule against hand-holding. It was an easy way to hurt a girl's feelings, an important thing to do with regularity. Just to keep them in their place.

"Yes, really," he said.

"But it's spelled differently," she said.

"They always make mistakes on statues. You didn't know that?"

"No," she said.

She was descended from German immigrants who had moved to the middle-of-nowhere Pennsylvania and opened filthy factories. Of course she didn't know that they always misspelled names of statues.

"How can you not know that? Everyone knows that," he said. He pushed her away and laughed. "You're showing your Pennsylvania Hun roots!"

FOR A WHILE, he had been pretending to go to class but instead he'd go to Newbury Street and loiter at Newbury

Comics, or hit up the cheap strip clubs in the Combat Zone with the money he made busing tables and selling some coke for Moses, if he didn't do it all with the strippers. This had worked for a while, but BC wasn't a huge campus by any means, so maybe Stephanie had figured something out. She never said anything to admit this knowledge. He forgot what she'd said. Something stupid. He'd showed up at her apartment at least a handful of times after she stopped returning his calls. And then he would think on his feet. It was both exciting and heartening to do so, until the last time. When it didn't work. Then he just got mad.

A part of him had known this day was coming so he'd stolen her Psychology 101 book two weeks earlier. He'd stolen this, and only this. It was a large hardcover textbook she kept around from her first semester of freshman year. It had collected some dust. She was not very clean, which he attributed to her being big and lazy, and rich, because rich people didn't clean. He'd assumed he could get away with it, and he was correct. She'd putz around her room looking for it, with her big lumbersome body, then she'd go do a once-around the shared living room.

"Where it is? What did I do with it?"

"Where is what?"

"My Psych 101 textbook."

He, as usual, was languishing on her bed, reading her handful of women's magazines. There was a new one out called *Sassy* that was purportedly more "feminist" than your standard fare. It was funny, because there was all this shit about clothes to make them sex objects and then there were articles about how they were not sex objects or something. It made no sense but it was a women's magazine, even a "girls'" magazine, so why would it. He flipped through, looking for jack-off material. His dick was a little hard, puffed up, so that was good.

He grunted and didn't look up.

He had perfected his father's grunt. It was a "not my problem," or, more to the point, a "what's your problem?" noise. Dismissive of its receiver, but one that also affirmed his masculinity. It was a deep grunt, a manly grunt.

But as her eyes became warier, and her body language became less friendly, he knew his time was running short.

"STOP STALKING ME."

"What?" She had just shut the front door of her building and he was waiting there. He rounded his shoulders and hung his head. He appeared to be searching his mind so he could understand. He even waved his arms around in confusion. "I don't understand," he said. "My father died. I need you." Then he made a small noise of sadness followed by a shrug of his shoulders. Then he looked right at her. He had puppy-dog eyes, he was told by many. "Do you want to get lunch?"

"No, I don't want to get lunch. Stop stalking me."

"What about tomorrow? Let's go to the Vietnamese place."

"No." In her hand she had a jacket and some socks he'd left there. Most of his stuff he'd gotten out with the psychology book, but he hadn't paid Moses rent in months and when he occasionally crashed on the couch and ran into Moses, it was starting to get ugly. Moses had rented his room out to a bass player with a drug problem from some local band that played the Rat once a week. He brought in a lot of customers. Doughty's time was nigh.

"Take these, or I'll throw them out," she said, handing him the jacket and socks. "Take them now, or I'm dropping them on the sidewalk. You're a creep."

AND THEN MOSES kicked him out. It was a bit unnerving, but he didn't take it personally. He was a Mexican, after all. Doughty collected all his stuff from the sidewalk. A small pile of clothes that had been on his mattress, a bag with some toiletries. He dusted off his pants. His elbow was bleeding from where he had hit the sidewalk. Leave it to a Mexican to ruin one of my shirts, he thought, and he pressed his, thankfully, dark-blue long-sleeved T-shirt against the wound to stanch the flow. Moses stood in the doorway. It was 6 A.M. and they both were coked up. Moses was in the door waving a knife around.

"*Puta madre*," Moses was yelling. "You stole my coke! You haven't paid rent in six months! I call the cops!"

Doughty laughed at him. He was in Doughty's country illegally. He had coke in the house! Well, he did before Doughty had taken it all less than twenty minutes ago. Moses wasn't going to call the cops. But Doughty was tired of the drama. It was time for his next move in life.

HE STUFFED HIS clothes into his backpack, strapped it on his wide-shouldered back, and decided it was time to move to New York City.

Chapter 8

Many ambitious BC grads moved to New York. He went straight to the Greyhound station and took the first bus to Port Authority. New York City, where his ancestors once owned big chunks of land, the private tales of negotiating with the heathens, giving them handfuls of beads and so on. Amazing what cleverness could do, and how it was passed down from generation to generation. He had a second cousin on his father's side who still owned a nice chunk of Fifth Avenue. That part of the family seemed to have lost touch with his part, and his mother said she really didn't know what he was talking about when he brought it up. He told her it had been her responsibility to find out things like this from his father before he'd died. He told her she was a serious disappointment. But the truth was, it wasn't a big concern to Doughty. He knew he'd find a way back to his rightful place. He'd meet the second cousin someday, maybe at a gala or private club, or maybe a roulette table in some other country, both of them in tuxes, meeting by pure chance. Or maybe the second cousin would seek him out, when he found out Doughty was in the city and all that he'd accomplished. Time was on his side. When he stepped off the bus, he was in the greatest city in the world. He was in the city that his people had made for their progeny to enjoy. He stood up straight, and walked northeast to the YMCA on East Forty-Seventh Street.

He had the $345 from his father's bank account in his wallet and probably $400's worth of cocaine. After renting the room for the night—he had the bottom bunk of one of the two bunk beds in the room—he took off his shoes, and lined them up neatly next to his backpack and stretched out on the bed. He'd unpack later.

He'd made it. He'd made it to the greatest city in the world. He was a resident of the Upper East Side, really the only neighborhood to live in, the neighborhood where he would find his kind. This thought relaxed him so much that he took a long, sound sleep. When he woke, it took a moment to get oriented. The light had faded. He'd slept so long and so well. He breathed a deep, easy breath and with his backpack on him, went to the hall bathroom. There were a couple of men lingering, but he had nothing to hide, nothing to be ashamed of. He peed. Then he went to the hall pay phone. First, he called Stanny. Stanny was living off campus in Burlington. They had exchanged numbers over the holidays. Doughty's little black address book was full of numbers, thanks to his dead dad and his own industriousness.

"Stan the Man!"

"Hey, Doughty."

"I moved to NYC. How goes it?"

"You're done with college?"

"I graduated early. You still have a year left?"

"This semester then yeah, a year."

"I was thinking of coming to Vermont to visit but I'm so busy right now. You should come to New York. We can par*tay!*"

"Where are you?"

"I'm on the Upper East Side. But thinking of moving downtown."

"What? What are you doing?"

"Real estate right now. Things are about to boom."

"The economy is shit, Doughty."

His quarter was running out and a large Black man was coming toward him.

"I'm getting a call about a rental. I mostly do sales but gotta take this. Talk soon."

HE LEFT THE Y with all of his belongings in his backpack and walked downtown to the East Village. The East Village and the West Village, also referred to broadly as "downtown Manhattan," were the places to buy drugs and gawk at the freaks. It was something all children from respectable families did. A rite of passage, if not a wonderful spree of freedom from all the responsibilities of their positions in society. It was night now. The walk took almost two hours—he didn't hurry—and was a great way to get some exercise while smoking. He sat on a bench in Tomkins Square Park. The remnants of Tent City were spread out over the park, some tented hovels remained or had been reinstated since the police takedown, and punk rock kids were everywhere, doing drugs, hanging out, and begging, many with their pit bulls. He was getting hungry.

He tried to arrange and collect thoughts that had been streaming around his mind. He did a little bump of coke. He did so with complete discretion. Then he did a bigger bump, stretching his thumb up and filling the cave-like spot between his wrist and knuckle with a nice white mound. That was it for now. He liked to show some self-control. He had so many good ideas, so many directions to go in. He was in NYC. The world was his oyster. The world was his. He was young and healthy and handsome. He ran his hands through his blond wavy locks. Shook them. He decided to go to a bar. Crossing the park, he passed a white woman, hair dyed blue, smoking in front of her tented pile of belongings with a pit bull on a dirty dog bed next to her. The flap to her tent was slightly open and inside he saw boxes, some small pieces of luggage, and a thin mattress pad. She asked him for change for dog food. She was a large girl with full lips and green eyes. Her cleavage was impressive, white and soft and pushing forward out of her black lace bra with a ripped-up Sex Pistols T-shirt covering it. She was high on something, or things.

"Can I have a cigarette?" he asked.

"I bummed this one, man."

"What's your name?"

"Amanda," she said.

Amanda, he thought. "Nice to meet you," Doughty said, and off he went. He'd made a new friend. A few blocks from Amanda's tent, on Avenue A, he saw a bar called Lucy's. He walked the length of the long bar and took a seat near the pool table in the back. An Eastern European woman was behind it and after his second beer, he learned that she was Lucy and she was Polish. The crowd was mostly young people, dressed similarly to Amanda. But there was also an older Mexican man who appeared to be very drunk sitting in the very far corner seat. And a well-dressed Black man came near him, holding on to a cue stick. The man ordered a Maker's on the rocks and his accent was Jamaican. Then he went off to the pool table.

Doughty sipped his beer. The bathrooms—one for women, one for men—were on his side of the pool table. In back was a door that must have led to an office, or a basement with an office in it. The walls were vinyl fake-wood paneling. A big cracked mirror hung behind the bar and another—even more cracked—on the opposite wall. Lucy was on a stool, dusting the liquor bottles on the top shelf. She had the beers in a sink full of ice. He liked this bar.

An older white woman came in and sat by the door. He glanced at her and then looked away. Doughty cataloged what he saw, continuing to watch her from his side-eye. She was thin—not his thing, but whatever—and had bleached blond hair, blue eyes, too much eyeliner, and money. Her purse looked like it was a Coach, and her wallet was nice, and she laid down a twenty. Lucy was kind and attentive. A regular. She drank vodka. She looked around and he felt her eyes on him. So, she liked younger men. She was in her mid-to-late forties? She hadn't had any work done. He'd seen women like her get big fake lips, or big fake tits, or do something really messed up with their eyes. She had decent genes. The booze was catching up with her, but she was still pulling it off.

He was in.

He gathered his thoughts, his observations, and took a nice, deep breath. He looked at her again and made eye contact. Then he stood and went to the bathroom, peed mostly to admire his dick, and did a bump. When he returned, she was ordering another drink.

Well, her first vodka had gone fast! Probably to get normal. He'd wait until she was on her third, then she'd get friendly. It wouldn't be long. He looked at his watch—he would time her drinks. It was a nice watch, a Hamilton that he'd taken before his dad was totally dead, a 1941 Boulton that had once belonged to his grandfather, and it would help with this situation. With any situation, really. It didn't scream money, but it also showed he wasn't a punk. Not that a little bit of his shabbiness wasn't an asset. It was 10 P.M. He was thinking on his feet now. He loved his ability to do that, to assess things correctly, understand how he was seen, how he presented himself to the world, see how the world saw him, as if he were standing outside himself, or even hovering above the whole room.

After her third vodka arrived she looked up at him and he smiled—lips over teeth, of course. She smiled back. After a few minutes he couldn't wait any longer. He wondered if he needed an excuse, but thinking on his feet he was, so on his feet he went, and he walked over with his beer and sat next to her.

"Hey, I've had a long day, how about you? I'm Doughty. I just moved here." He put out his hand for her to shake, and she took it. Her hand was nicely delicate. A big ring with a green stone on her forefinger.

It worked. She was flattered. A woman alone at a bar on her third drink will always appreciate the attentions of a young, handsome man.

"Moving is exhausting." Good. She showed him empathy. He loved this about women. It was their job to comfort and they knew it. "Where are you from?"

"Boston." Up close he saw that he had guessed her age correctly, more or less. The lighting was incredibly dim. His side-eye caught his own image in the cracked mirror. He saw himself in it, it refracted his face and broad shoulders into different parts. Then he homed in on her. He was guessing, surmising, allowing himself room to assess, to make some mistakes. But he was focused. Razor-sharp focused. "I got a job after college." He smiled and did the head tilt. Here, he showed his cards a bit. He admitted his age.

"Well that's exciting," she said, coolly. "What's the job?"

"I'm in real estate for the time being."

"What do you want to do?"

"I'm going to graduate school for psychology in the fall."

"Oh, wow. Where?" She finished her third vodka.

"NYU."

"Are you taking out loans?"

"No. God no. I'll be teaching. I got a full ride."

"That's exciting." She stared off dully at the long rows of bottles of alcohol behind the bar.

"What do you do?" Then he laughed lightly. "I know, such a cliché question."

"It's okay," she said. This was good. The bottomless pit of the need to comfort. This impulse was a good one, one he could feed from, nurse. Doughty had scored already, he knew it. "I'm an editor."

"What kind of an editor," he asked.

"I work at Little, Brown," she said.

This got tricky. He had no idea what Little, Brown was. But he betrayed nothing. He just nodded knowingly. It was important not to be impressed. But it was also important to be knowledgeable.

"You've heard of it?"

"Of course," he said.

She smiled. Then she started talking and they kept drinking, and she paid the bill, and he learned everything about her.

She was, of course, drunker than him when she opened the large, heavy door to the building of her loft on Mercer Street in SoHo. Doughty helped her swing it out, noting its heft. The building, a converted industrial building, was clearly not made for living in. One thing she didn't mention was family money, but he was assuming she had some, as she didn't make a lot as an editor—that she did reveal. She had even complained how little it was for the work she did. No one could afford a loft like this, even if downtown was funky and cheaper than pretty much anywhere besides the outer boroughs, if they didn't have some money.

THE NEXT MORNING, Sophia was very hungover, so hungover that she wanted sex again. Her body, although not young, was somewhat manageable. Yes, he did close his eyes and concentrate on other things. Beata's mouth had been sort of permanently stuck in his head now for years as a backup plan when he was getting bored with Stephanie's tits, for instance. She was naked, as was he, and he slid down to her cunt and went to work. Up and down with the tongue, circles. She tasted clean, vodka did that, but there was some animal dankness to it. He let his tongue go flat. Pulling away, leaning in, gentle, gentle. Then he'd slam into it. He was about to pull back and do the alphabet, but she was close. She had been too drunk last night to even try to come, he had just banged away at her for a while, not even coming himself, but now he had her. Soon, he grabbed her thighs as she went bonkers on him. When the hurricane of her orgasm ended, he fell onto his back and breathed.

Then she got up and walked to the bathroom and he took in the backside of her. It wasn't so bad. She still had a waist.

The loft was not soundproof. The floors creaked, which was charming, but then the sound of her peeing in the only bathroom was not. He had to take a dump. He put on his pants and walked toward the front of the loft, to the windows that looked down on Prince Street. In that space were a small living room setup, a desk, and endless bookshelves, as well as books piled up on the floor against the walls. It was a lovely, bright warm day, and people were starting to emerge. She came out of the bathroom in a small silk-looking beige nightie. It was nice. At least she wasn't fat. Although she could gain some weight. But at her age, it would probably go to all the wrong places. Like her stomach.

A flat stomach. Now there was something to enjoy in life. Hers wasn't quite that, but it wasn't a stomach that had its own personality, like Stephanie's tits, and that was a good thing.

"My turn," he said, and smacked her ass just a tad too hard as he walked to the bathroom.

"Hey!" she said. She looked at him, red-eyed, a bit confused. "Ouch."

He smiled at her. "Every woman loves a fascist!" He had learned that from his father.

She looked confused for a beat, then laughed.

Making people think something true was just a joke was something he kept perfecting and perfecting. It was a favorite tool.

After he took a huge shit, he looked in the bathroom cabinet. In it were a bunch of lady things—tampons, various ointments, makeup. After glancing around those, he went to the medications and it was a gold mine. There was Xanax, Prozac—no Ritalin, sadly. The Xanax bottle was full, so he took two. Even though he had planned on selling the coke, he decided to snort up two decent-size lines on the lovely marble bathroom counter in celebration of his new friendship with Sophia.

The shower was very large—no tub—and had a dark-gray cement floor. This was a thing he squirreled away in his head. This look. He got naked, showered, lingering and enjoying it. Fancy soaps wrapped in delicately folded papers with French words on them, and shampoos and conditioners in sleek, angular bottles, the caps firmly closed. Wrapping himself in a towel from the rack of towels—they were thick and heavy, off-white—he walked back out. The floors were rough on his feet. People and their fashions, he thought. He grunted to himself. She needed to get her floors done. They should be smooth.

He walked toward the back of the loft, the bedroom and living room behind him, into the open kitchen area, which had a window that faced a cement courtyard, and a fire escape. The loft was a little over two thousand square feet. Besides the bathroom and the small bedroom, there were no enclosed spaces, and the loft retained that loft feeling. He was starting to understand the logic of this, of open space. He sat down at a small wooden table with four mismatched chairs— a thing? Eclectic? Sophia came from the front, a cup of coffee in her hand.

"You showered," she said. "How was it?" Already searching for a compliment.

He grunted. "The cement floor is rough."

He watched her face fall.

"I know, it's all the rage now, cement bathrooms," she said sheepishly. Good.

He grunted again. It was funny. His father had left him many gifts. He had the grunt, for one. A Hamilton watch.

"Do you want milk or sugar?" Now she was facing the kitchen, getting him a coffee. He could get used to this.

"Milk."

Music was playing on a sleek black player, which in shape reminded him of his toolbox, although much smaller, a rectangular box with a radio and a CD component. A woman, singing. He flinched. "What is this music?"

"It's Kate Bush." She looked at him, searchingly. He loved a hungover person. They were confused about the night before, so then they became confused about everything: the music they love, their bathroom floors. He didn't say anything. This, too, was so powerful. Silence. In many ways, silence was the verbal equivalent to being still. To standing your ground. To being firm. In charge. If you don't give anything to someone, you are in control. The caffeine was kicking in with the lines of coke. He felt great. He had stuck to beer, so besides taking a huge shit, he was fine. He looked around. He liked it here. It was a step down from the Upper East Side, but SoHo was coming up in the world. It was changing. Plus, it had a cool vibe that might have been lost on some Darien and Boston College people, but he was ahead of the game. Always good to be a step ahead.

She turned off the music. She blabbed about how she had things to do. Manuscripts to read.

"So that was fun. But I have to work."

"How long have you lived here?"

"A few years."

"Where is your office?"

"Little, Brown is in Midtown." She had told him that last night, but he was making conversation. She didn't remember shit. He would look up her work address later.

He got up and poured himself another coffee. "What sort of books do you edit?"

"Fiction and nonfiction."

She seemed antsy. Maybe he should fuck her again. He liked it here. He walked over to her. She was standing. He put his hand between her legs. She was still wet. He wondered if he could get her to sing again. He got hard. He could bang her like mad, which although that would not make her come, it would make her, well, banged.

"Listen, I have work."

But she was giving in. He felt it as she moved her cunt toward his hand.

"It's the weekend!"

"I know, but I have a lot to do for tomorrow. I work weekends, sadly."

He sighed and removed his hand from her cunt and walked to the front of the loft, toward her desk and living room area, and the sun was bright but not too bright. They were high enough, four floors high, so as not to hear the noise on the street, although it was a fairly quiet block. He sat down at her desk. She was following him at this point. "This is where you work?" He grunted.

"Yes."

"Ha!" he said.

She had papers on her desk and a bulletin board above it, and the large window looking out on Prince Street was to the side. The bulletin board was full of scribbled notes. He pointed at them. "What is that mess?" He laughed heartily now. This garbage was beyond a grunt. It deserved a larger reaction.

"Those are notes. I'm editing a novel and I have a deadline. It's fascinating. Postmodern, very digressive."

"Ha!" He stood and put his hands around her waist, sliding them down to her hips. They were small hips, encasing her medium-size pouch of a stomach. She moved in closer to him.

"Why 'ha'?"

"Ha," he said again, pulling his head back, but tightening his grip on her hips.

Her face was unsmiling.

"Listen, you've got to go. I have to work." She put her face to his neck. "You're distracting me."

"I can be *not* distracting." He pulled away. "Do you mind if I smoke?"

"You can smoke off the kitchen on the fire escape."

He had to climb out the window—it was very doable, but it wasn't a door. He looked into the courtyard and lit a cigarette. He could see into the neighbors' window. It was a kitchen as well. There seemed to be no access to it from where he smoked. He could walk down the fire escape and then there was a big jump. The neighbor didn't have a fire escape to climb up. No one was in there, but the shades weren't drawn. He loved smoking and he felt if he could smoke more, eventually he'd get more information about her neighbors. After about twenty minutes, she came into the kitchen.

"I really need you to go."

"Did you get any work done?"

"I mean, yeah, but it would be easier if you weren't here."

He climbed back into the kitchen. "I need to use the bathroom."

"Okay," she said, and although she was visibly agitated, he wasn't ready to give up. In fact, it was important not to let her mood affect him, but to note it anyway.

When he came out another twenty minutes later, having chewed another Xanax, she was drinking a vodka on the couch in the living room next to the desk area. He stretched in front of her, and ran his fingers through his hair.

"I need you to leave."

He yawned. He really wanted a nap from those Xanax.

She walked to the door and opened it. This pissed him off. He sat down on the couch.

"Get out."

He stood up and said, "I just can't get enough of you. Looking at you."

She blushed. "I'll see you soon. But I have to work."

He decided it was time to switch gears. Make her want him. As he left, he could see she was going in for a kiss, but he pulled his head back and just left, hearing her say goodbye to his back as he headed down the stairs. He said nothing. She had given him her phone number the night before, written it down in his address book. And he knew where to find her.

HE WALKED BACK to the East Village. It was about 3 P.M. The success of meeting Sophia heartened him. It didn't surprise him, but it proved him right about himself. He had money, he had cocaine, he had a loft in SoHo. He decided to eat. He saw a dumpy diner called the Kiev and went in and had eggs. Then he meandered about. So many choices! It was late in the afternoon now, so he went into a bar that reminded him of Lucy's from the outside. The Cherry Tavern. And behind the bar, lo and behold, was Beata.

Chapter 9

Beata. It took maybe half a second to verify in his mind that it was actually her. Her hair was dyed black and cut all choppy with a generous amount of gel spiking it all around her bird head. Her nose was pierced. But there she was. It almost made him believe in miracles, or luck, but then he remembered that life was full of opportunities and it was just a question of handling them correctly.

She watched him walk up to the bar and her wide mouth opened and then shut tight. What a coincidence that her mouth had been on his mind just last night. Well, it was usually on his mind when his dick got hard, which was often. It sometimes bothered him, or sort of amused him, but it was what it was.

"Beata," he said. "I was just thinking of you! And here you are. Wow!" He sat down, and noted that the barstools were good ones with backs. He couldn't stand the stools with no backs, the little round things to perch on. Those were so not inviting. It was a smaller bar than Lucy's, but with the same fake-wood paneling. There were colorful antique-looking framed beer advertisements on the walls. It was cozier because it was smaller. Maybe it reminded Beata of her house. There were two other men sitting at the bar on the far side, near a pool table. Doughty sat at the corner curve near the door, near the sinks, where she had been washing glasses.

"Doughty," she said.

Somewhat understandably, she didn't seem as happy as he'd have liked her to be, seeing him there. He'd make it right. She was, despite everything, lucky to know a man like him. They were grown-ups now, grown-ups in the big city.

"We found each other!" he said. "Can I get a Rolling Rock?"

She pulled one out of a sink of ice. She looked good. She looked the same in many ways. She was tall and spindly and in place of her bright, tight clothing, she was encased in black, somewhat loose clothing. Her T-shirt was artfully ripped and hung loosely on her shoulders, showing her black lace bra straps on her pale, bony shoulders. Her look, not surprisingly, was similar to the tent-living, dog-owning woman. Amanda, that was her name. He was good with names. In fact, after he crossed the Bowery, it was as if the uniform for women had changed. They all had ripped T-shirts, they all wore black. He couldn't tell if her bra was padded still. It looked like it might not be. Change is normal. The nose ring was ugly, but she *was* from Waterbury.

"What are you doing here?" she asked, bar rag in hand. Just like she was in Watertown, ready to clean up and serve.

"I moved here a few weeks ago," he said. He didn't like her tone. "What are *you* doing here?"

"I moved here two years ago."

"Ha!" he said. "No one gets out of Waterbury."

She looked at him. "I did."

"And here you are," he said, and with his hand did a sweeping motion around the bar. Although it was like Lucy's, it smelled sort of bad. Like rat feces? Probably because it wasn't owned by a Polish woman who cleaned a lot. The vinyl floor looked lumpy. It definitely must have felt like home to her.

"What do you want, Doughty?"

Things hadn't gone perfectly well with Beata. But this serendipitous moment was meaningful. A great feeling of fortune rose in him. It was almost too much. "Can I have a shot of Maker's, too?"

She turned around to get the bottle and chose a tiny shot glass instead of a rocks glass.

"That's five dollars."

He was going to laugh, then he thought about grunting, but that didn't seem quite right. He decided on a look of confusion. Yes, the wide-eyed "awe shucks what's wrong" look.

The rudeness of asking for money was a sign she was still upset with him. Therefore it also was a sign she still had feelings for him. Being upset was a feeling. In Boston, he'd learned that the tiny shot glasses were for drunk college kids. He had some bartender friends from his time in the restaurant industry. He knew what was what.

He lifted the baby shot glass like it was a strange object, looking at it askance. "What's this?"

"It's a shot."

"Beata, see those men down there?" He spoke quietly and nodded in their direction. "They are drinking real shots."

"That's five dollars," she said again. She put a hand on her hip. Squirreled her mouth around into something that was not quite a pout. It was too hard.

"Beata," he said. He took out a tenner and put it on the table. It was time for him to be magnanimous. "Keep the change."

She said nothing. How ungrateful. He downed the shot.

"What time do you get off work?" he asked. "I feel like running into you here is deep, Beata. Let's catch up. I know things got a little strange at the end of high school . . ."

"You whored me out to your friends," she said.

"Wow, careful." He leaned forward. And glanced at the end of the bar. From his side-eye, he noticed the men paying attention. "They could have heard that."

"Those guys are my regulars. And I didn't do anything wrong."

"Well, you blew my friends."

She gave him a look.

"I mean, you didn't say *no*."

This got her. She hadn't said no. She'd blown them. He hadn't put a gun to her head. Yes, he brought her over to Lew's house, and yes, he had planned the entire thing. But she didn't walk out. She was escorted—agreed, she was a little confused—into Lew's bedroom and did Lew first and then when Lew came out and Stanny went in, as he recalled, it didn't go well.

"What do you want," she said again. Her nails were painted,

something the lower classes did, even if they were going to get chipped. It was such a tell, painted nails. She had a rag in her hand and was wiping the bar angrily with it. Born to clean, he noted.

He supposed he had to do the act-of-contrition thing. He leaned his head to one shoulder, made a sad face. "I was a dumb kid. Let me make it up to you."

He got her. Her eyes softened a bit. An apology. It was so easy. "I'm really sorry, Beata. I was a kid."

"I lost my virginity to you," she said quietly. "I thought you liked me. Then you did that."

"It was special, I did like you," he said. "I *do* like you. And now we're both in New York. Where do you live? Can I have a real shot?"

He saw her agitation. He was fairly certain her hands were shaking, not like Sophia's, not from lack of alcohol, but from emotion.

"Let me buy you a shot, Beata. And myself a real one." He hated spending money on stupid things, but sometimes, he had to gamble a bit.

"Let's see the money," she said.

Wow. She didn't trust him. Okay. He put a twenty on the bar. She looked at it, then at him, then poured them both shots. Real shots, replacing his college-boy shot glass with a real glass, a lowball glass. He took out another ten, and they did another round. She was calming down. Alcohol was good at that.

"I really like the hair, Beata." She touched it then, a good thing, like following his directions. "You were always so cool."

Then he noticed the red heart around her neck. She still had it. He said, "Tell me all about yourself! You're such a rock star." And then it flowed.

She lived in Brooklyn, and he had no idea what that meant. But she was getting an apartment on Mulberry Street, in Little Italy, because she also tended bar at a place called Milady's in SoHo on the corner of Prince and Thompson. So, she was going to be Sophia's neighbor. Well, SoHo was full of huge lofts and Little Italy was full of tiny tenement buildings from when the Wops were new to America. Yet here she was, blablaing about how excited she was to move into a tenement apartment. The building was owned by a friend of the third-generation Italian family who owned Milady's, and they were helping her get out of Brooklyn. Where she lived wasn't safe. But she paid only $350 a month for her room. She had three roommates. It was off the F train, the Bergen Street stop. But she rarely took the train because it didn't run with any regularity and it was dangerous, so she took gypsy cabs, because yellow cabs wouldn't go to Brooklyn.

"I'm getting my RN at Pace College," she said. Finally she stopped talking after that. She almost seemed proud of her sad, menial-labor life. She went down to the other end of the bar and he could see her serving the two men, and then she turned and looked back at him. Now she was talking about him to *them*. He looked at them through his side-eye. One was not too old, had shaggy, longish brown hair, nothing distinct about him. The other was thick and red-faced and staring at him. His eyes were very blue and very shiny, the wet-eyed, glowy effect of alcohol.

Doughty was so glad she had finally stopped talking about herself. All information about a person's life was a helpful tool, even if her life had been and still was cheap. His father had once given him a very long sermon-like speech on how most human lives were cheap. Easy to buy, easy and not a big deal to dispose of, this was the vast majority of human life on the planet and the history of civilization. Like a crop of corn, cut them down, eat them up, and wait for the next season of growth, then do it again. And that reality was what helped make his family what it was. It was just a fact, an unchangeable fact of existence. One to be embraced.

She walked back to the sink. Sitting by the sink was a great idea, because she would have to come back to wash glasses.

"You know, while I'm closing on my deal to buy this house in the West Village, I would love to see where you live. I'm temporarily living on the Upper East Side." He took a beat. "I could make you feel safer there."

"I don't think so. You're in real estate?"

"Yes, yes, it's a great time for it, a buyer's market. What time do you get off?"

"Four."

"Four A.M.?"

"Yeah. I'm working a double today. We open at two P.M. on the weekends. How long have you been in New York? Bars are open until four A.M."

"I'll pick you up."

"Let me think about it," she said. There was doubt there. But he wasn't worried. He wasn't a quitter. She was vulnerable and he was strong. It was a no-brainer.

He stood up. "I'll be here for you," he said, and as her hand was on the bar, he took this as a sign and put his large hand over her little one. She pulled it away. But it didn't matter. She had felt his strength. He would help her. He was always helping. He would help her feel safe in scary, dangerous Brooklyn.

FIRST HE WALKED back to SoHo, to check on what Sophia was doing. He stood across from her building. He smoked and paced a bit. It was a nice bonus that she didn't have a doorman. Next to her building, a new hotel, the Mercer, had just opened up. It had large windows all along the bottom floor. He surmised it was some sort of lounge area. He watched men in black pants and black button-down shirts busying themselves around low tables, each one surrounded by black-cushioned chairs. He thought, This is classy, this is of the time. Sleek, black furniture. Monochrome, that was the word.

He looked up and saw Sophia's shadow by the window in the living room. She was in some sort of dressing gown and it reminded him of his mother's robe.

He lit a cigarette. Then Sophia came down, struggling with the heavy front door of the industrial building. She was so slight in many ways. He thought about helping her and then thought, Nah. It was important to parcel out his help. He didn't want someone to think they *deserved* his kindness. His kindness was always a gift. A beautiful, rare gift to be treasured and never taken for granted.

"Oh hey, Sophia!" He smiled with lips open. He thought it

was necessary, even though he mostly hid his teeth, but there were moments when an open-mouthed smile was useful. It showed enthusiasm—maybe surprise. Honesty.

"What are you doing here?" she asked.

"I'm meeting friends for dinner."

She was wearing her dressing gown outside. Her thin hair was pulled back in an orange scarf. It made her look like a cancer victim, but he decided to hold that thought for another moment, when explaining how the scarf made her look like a dying old person would be more appropriate.

"Nice headscarf. A little bright."

"They don't serve dinner until six. It's four-thirty P.M."

"The lounge is open." Palm facing upward, he gently motioned to the windows. "We're meeting early for a drink. How was work?"

"It's fine. I'm just running an errand."

He threw his cigarette in the gutter and moved toward her, standing very close. She didn't move away.

"Last night was so fun," he said. Then he articulated some more. "You were amazing."

This made her blush, or rather made the vodka in her face come forward. She took a step back. "What friends?"

"Friends from my real estate business. Partners, really." He breathed deeply, and his chest opened up and swelled. "Work never ends." He smiled, this time with lips closed, shaking his head slightly, oh the endless grind of real estate in New York City. "Real estate," he said. "It's 24/7."

She was examining him. But he knew after two more drinks or so she'd lose that thought.

"Yeah." She smiled then, softening toward him. Probably remembering her huge orgasm. Now they had the commonality of working hard. New Yorkers, he thought, we're all the same. "Okay. I gotta go," she said.

"See you soon." He didn't want to be too forward, so he skipped leaning in for a kiss.

"Sure." she said. "That would be nice. Call me."

"I will," Doughty said.

"Yeah, okay, I have to go." And off she went.

As she walked away, she did a little wave and said, "Bye." He noticed her hand, and focused for a moment on the size of the rings on her fingers. Both had large stones, one looked turquoise, and the other was the green one from last night, both so heavy they slid to the side of her fingers with their weight. She slouched, which was unfortunate. A slouching woman in her forties, in a dressing gown, unshowered, clomping around in clogs. Probably going to buy more vodka.

Then under his breath, he said, "237-4463" over and over again as he walked in the other direction. He had it written down, but it was fun to memorize. Good for the brain muscle. After a couple of blocks, he was saying it louder and this wasn't good. People were around. He found a bench, sat down. He thought about her clogs. Her clogs really got him. They grossed him out, which made him angrier. He could stoop only so low without feeling the need to make a correction. The clogs had to go.

But the loft. "Think of the loft, Doughty," he said to himself. He turned east and walked to Second Avenue. He was heading uptown, but first he passed the Cherry Tavern, for good luck. From the other side of the street, he could see into the bar. There was his black-haired Beata. Then he kept going uptown. He was rich with possibilities. He was on the right path.

Chapter 10

He passed most of the evening walking around. It was good for his stamina. He was so happy to be in the city. It really was the best city in the world, New York. He hummed to himself—*if you can make it here, you can make it everywhere*—imaging Liza Minnelli in tight tiny, little shorts, singing on stage, balancing expertly on five-inch heels. Sparkling. He knew she was a gay icon, but she was hot. She was rich, talented. Really rich. She was royalty. And she didn't wear clogs.

He realized he was hungry. At a bodega on Second Avenue, he bought a bunch of tuna cans and a loaf of Wonder bread and went back to the Y. After he ate in his bunk, he napped.

Napping was an underrated life skill. He could close his eyes anywhere, at any time, let go of the world and go into a deep, profound rest. His father had been the same, a man with an incredible gift for the dreamless, deep sleep. Doughty was so in tune with his body, like his father, he could command it to rest and command it to be virile and work. He had amazing control over both his body and his mind. It was an inherited gift. A genetic gift. But also, he thought, as he drifted back to a waking state, in the lovely space between sleep and wakefulness, one he honed with his hard work. With his practice of body control.

When he woke, fully, it was almost one in the morning. After he admired his Hamilton watch a little more, he stretched and did the math. He had a little over three hours to get to the Cherry Tavern. There was a ruckus going on in the hall and he knew that it had probably been going on for some time, but he had shut it all out. His great genetic ability to take care of his body, his body being a machine he'd honed well with will and power. Genes weren't anything unless you worked hard to harness and nurture them. He hadn't noticed the noise until now and this was a good thing. A white man came in and sat on the bottom bunk next to him and said something to him. Doughty pointed to his ears and said, "I am depf." He nodded his head downward and to one side. The guy grunted, but not like Doughty's grunt. It was a weak, higher-pitched grunt. Happily, it was time to go get Beata at a decidedly leisurely pace. Like napping, taking one's time was far better than being hurried and was another skill he'd perfected. Never let people rush you. Stay in charge.

Before he left, he packed his possessions in his backpack, then headed to the bathrooms. A stall next to the urinals was open, so he went in and snorted two big bumps. It was a little extravagant, but why not? He deserved it.

He walked. His bag was getting lighter, and he gently shook the coke, then folded it up neatly into itself. He wasn't a fan of the subway. He could feel his calves getting stronger, his glutes tightening. Walking was so underrated. He decided to take a small detour to Grand Central Station as a way to enjoy his unhurried stroll.

Grand Central had been his gateway to NYC during high school. So many memories of just trying to get out of the crumbling, smelly, dark building with petty thieves and Black people and so forth hanging around, getting directly into a taxi with his Darien friends to be whisked away to a Park Avenue penthouse to do blow in some grandparents' empty apartment, grandparents who were in the Alps skiing or something. And maybe that had happened only once or twice, he hadn't kept count, but Grand Central had still made an impression on him, an impression of decay and danger.

When he got there, not much had changed. It had been only a few years, so no surprise. But he, Doughty, had changed. He was a New Yorker now, and he felt a different relationship to Grand Central. The glory of the building was still there, the incredible domed ceiling, the arched hallways. It was built in 1913 in the Beaux Arts style by Reed and Stem, and it covered over forty-eight acres. He had read all about it in the encyclopedia. It was a landmark building, but one that needed a shit ton of work. Many other people besides Reed and Stem had contributed to it as the years passed. He couldn't wait to get a little more settled, then he'd pick up his encyclopedias from his mother's place. He missed them.

He stood in the nearly empty main concourse of Grand Central, the place where, during the day, everyone came and went from the suburbs. It was a powerful feeling, as if he owned it. It was monumental. It was seedy. It had changed and changed again, but it was still a near emblem of New York, the entry and exit place of people who needed and deserved the calm and quiet and peace of the suburbs, yet worked in the city, the city that never sleeps, the city that stays the same but always changes. He slowed his pace, looking up slightly. It was very late, or very early, depending on one's perspective. And here he was, having this grand building all to himself, as if it belonged to him. His skin came alive. He wanted to invest in it! Oh, the glory!

He walked down a long hallway toward the men's room. On his way, he passed a few young men standing outside, leaning on the wall, smoking. He decided against joining them and walked straight into the cavernous men's toilets. Inside, he noted two older men in suits, drunk, standing at the sink, talking in low voices to each other. The echoes in Grand Central, even in the men's room, were something else. The entire room whispered to itself. He went to the urinals, but through his side-eye he saw the gentlemen turning and looking at him. He believed greatly in hydration, so he had drunk generously at the water fountain before he left the Y. Naps, he thought, while he started to urinate, made him thirsty. He heard the men come toward him. One was stifling a giggle, then he saw the other man right next to him. Doughty was on full display. He heard the slightest "oh" and he took an extra-long time shaking his dick and slowly, lovingly, he put it back, zipped his pants.

Then, very brief eye contact. Some words. He walked to the toilet stalls. The noises were hard to track, but he found an empty one and knew that the echoes behind him were from the heels of well-loved, well-worn, well-taken-care-of Oxford shoes. He left the stall door open. One of the men, thin and bald, with a gray suit, came in after him.

There was always something important about the first time. And there was always a first time for everything. It came so naturally to Doughty, and his awareness of how naturally he adjusted to new situations, his incredible ability to be so professional and at ease when taking on a new experience, energized him. He loved success. He was made for success.

So it was. Doughty sat down and haggled a bit, then got slightly menacing, which helped. He pulled his dick out and the touch of his own hand hardened it. The man wanted to talk and Doughty thought about hitting him, but he'd probably like it too much, so he refrained—his self-control was extraordinary—and, as the financial part was over, he wanted to make the rest as quick as possible. Time was money.

The man got on his knees and went to work and Doughty leaned back. At first he thought of closing his eyes and thinking of something while the man worked away. He then realized that closing his eyes was a bad idea. His hard-on *was* lagging, which made the man try harder and also pull away to say something, which Doughty did not want to happen. So he just lifted his butt up and shoved his dick deeper into the man's mouth and this shut him up. This went on for a while. He had a pocket full of cash, up front. He had his entire life ahead of him. Power surged through him and his dick got really hard. It was then he noticed the other man looking through the crack.

"Twenty dollars to come in and watch," he said. The other man pushed in—the door hadn't been locked—and shut it behind him and pulled out his small, red, crooked penis and started yanking at it. The sight of that distracted Doughty but then he pushed the head of the kneeling man away from his dick and said, "Twenty dollars."

After that was in his pocket, they all got in position again and it didn't take long. At first, the feel of the man's mouth bothered him, as did the bald head, which, because of his amazing vision, even though now he was looking straight ahead at the white bathroom door, he could see. The feel of his particularly thin saliva and his dryish, old-man lips. But he used the distraction, this irritation, as fuel. It was disgust really, and it made him angry, which made him harder. Anger was fuel to get the work done. Efficiency was one of his many skills. Toward the end, he did have to push the other man away once and say, "You watch only." He also said "Shut up" at least once. But this was the price of being the boss. You had to make rules clear.

There was no reason to dillydally, to prolong things.

AFTER THE BUSINESS was over, they all walked to the sinks, where a handful of older and younger men were talking in low voices. Someone smoked from a glass pipe and passed it to his friend.

As he and his consorts washed their hands, one brought out a flask and offered it to him, which he took and drank empty. The other had a small brown vile and sniffed it and offered it to Doughty. He'd tried it once in high school. Rush, it was called. Or poppers. It would be a nice little boost for his walk downtown. The man smiled. The smile was so generous that Doughty thanked him, keeping the bottle to himself. Then he had a thought. "Do you guys want some good stuff?" He got two hundred dollars out of them, and kept a little stash of the coke for himself.

IT WAS A lovely night. Second Avenue was quiet as he strolled downtown, but some bars had small groups of drunk people outside. The homeless occasionally asked him for money. He'd been careful not to look too well dressed. Knowing NYC as he did, he didn't want to draw too much attention to himself. He took occasional sniffs from his bottle. He felt amazing. He was going to see an old friend. To help an old friend. To help Beata.

Chapter 11

He got to Cherry Tavern, according to his Hamilton, at 3:40 A.M. She was closing up the bar. There was one man there, one he recognized from earlier. He was the shiny blue-eyed man. Out of his side-eye, he examined him a bit more. He was really big, a barrel-chested type, and coarse-haired. He smiled at Doughty, showing a mouth empty of front teeth. Just the fangs to either side of where his front teeth should have been.

Beata looked tired and annoyed. "I thought you weren't coming."

"I got held up on a complication for a deal," he said. "Here I am."

"A deal late at night? Seriously, Doughty."

She finished up at the register and walked around the bar, patting the man.

"Doughty, this is Joe Bird. He's mostly a regular of mine at Milady's. But he comes and checks in on me here."

She took a seat at one of the few tables next to the bar. She had a large pour of Maker's and was counting her tips.

Doughty took a moment. Should he even acknowledge Joe Bird? What kind of name was that? He decided to smile coolly, but not make eye contact. "Hey."

"Hiya, Dotty," Joe said. He drank half his Budweiser in one swig. Must be because of the no front teeth, Doughty thought. Interesting.

"It's 'Doughty,'" he said, and decided to honor Joe Bird with a brief, straight-up look at him.

"Gotcha, DOTTY," Joe repeated.

So he was too stupid to understand English and maybe his disfigured mouth hole didn't help. It was time to give up. Doughty joined Beata at the table and did his dreamy look. He practiced all sorts of looks in the mirror. This one, he rarely used. Being able to know how and when to configure his face in a certain manner was a skill that children didn't have. Men, real men, knew how the world saw them, so beyond seeing other people for what they were worth, controlling how you were seen was a survival skill, showing what you needed to show. It was more than just learning poker face. But it was related to poker face. He leaned toward Beata.

"It's true what they say about real estate, it's a 24/7 job in this market. But here I am! I am so exhausted, but I made it here."

She smiled a doubtful smile, and counted away. She had made almost three hundred dollars. In one night. Wow. He saw Joe with his beer coming toward them.

"Bee, you sure you don't need me to see you in a cab?"

Doughty stood then. "I got it, man." Bee. She had a nick-name.

"Thanks, Joe, I'm okay. See you at Milady's?"

"You got it, baby," he said, taking the bottle with him as he left. Then, with Doughty by her side, they left. He watched her lock up. She pulled down a metal gate over the front door and then secured it with a padlock. Where was the key? Doughty needed more poppers, the bottle he had had lost its potency. Was his focus waning? He didn't see what she did with the key, or if she even had it. Yet he knew it didn't matter, so he could dismiss this moment. There would be more moments. Patience was a virtue. Waiting was a virtue. Chances would come, if you just stayed around.

He didn't know what a gypsy cab was, but she did. They stood on Second Avenue and a black unmarked sedan slowed down and they got in. He watched her argue a bit about which way to go. He was impressed with how the driver bullied her for no reason and found it interesting as well to watch her, her overly tall, still terribly thin body behave all tough. It was the Waterbury in her, he realized. She knew what to do, it appeared, so he sat back and did nothing, just watched her get bullied while she held her ground. It was a fine time to delegate responsibility. The drive over the Brooklyn Bridge was quite lovely. He felt glad he had accomplished this, not that it would necessarily impress his friends. In fact, he was certain it wouldn't. Still. All experiences were to be squirreled away and all had value. And the drive over the bridge gave an exquisite view of Manhattan. Indeed, it was the best view ever, better than the views Manhattan gave of, say, Queens from the East Side, or New Jersey from the West Side. It was stunning.

She didn't let him fuck her and he didn't try too hard. He was tired. But he was in bed with her. And he had washed his dick in the sink beforehand, thinking he'd perform again. He wrapped his arm around her poky shoulders. Despite her hard angles, after Sophia he appreciated the damp firmness of her youthful skin. She was a young woman, and that was something. She smelled, even after working all day, fresh and new, the smell of a young person. She had her back turned to him. His dick got hard and he pressed it against her underwear. He put a finger in them, the yellow cotton panties, and pulled at them.

"Stop," she said, and then her breath changed. She was falling asleep.

It was, at this point, 5 A.M. His body was ready to rest again, so he rolled away from her. Her bed was a disgrace, but at least there was enough room to be in it without *having* to touch her. He grunted.

"What's this," he asked, patting the bed. He pulled at his dick.

"It's a futon." Her voice was very sleepy.

He grunted again. "What in God's name is a futon?"

"Doughty, I'm beat, I've been working all night. Let's talk tomorrow." She was basically slurring with sleep.

"I'm tired from working all night, too, Beata. Or should I call you Bee?" She was actually fading. "And taking you out here was something else. But I'm happy to do it for you." He waited for her gratitude, but she was asleep.

He looked at her next to him, lifting the cheap blue-checked polyester quilt, which was very light. He preferred a blanket with some weight. He realized he really preferred his loft with Sophia. And it bothered him that she wasn't naked. She even had on an undershirt, a white wifebeater, one that could be purchased at Rite Aid. As if she had anything to hide. She still didn't have any breasts. That hadn't changed, unlike her hair—or her demeanor. Her demeanor wasn't the same. She had something like confidence? It was annoying but nothing insurmountable. Come to think of it, she'd always had an attitude. Which came from where? Waterbury?

His pillow was okay. It had a nice amount of support, but wasn't overly fluffy. Overly fluffy pillows hurt his neck. He looked at the walls. There were some black-and-white photos taped to the door of her room. He was so tired, but he wished he had one of Sophia's Xanax. In the corner of her tiny room— he'd give her shit about how small it was later—on top of milk crates, was a board with colors on it, and next to it was a stack of some white blank things. Even though he had amazing vision, he couldn't see exactly what they were. Despite the dark sheets she had in the window facing the street—she lived above a laundromat and on a corner—there seemed to be some light flowing in. He breathed in and exhaled. Then he slept.

WHEN HE HEARD her get up and open the unlocked door of her room and walk up the creaky stairs to the second floor of the apartment, he opened his eyes. He looked at his Hamilton watch. It was seven minutes after noon. This was early. He closed his eyes and went back to sleep.

"Doughty? Doughty, wake up," she said. "I have to be somewhere soon."

He was almost always adding new information to the vast and powerful file in his brain, but sometimes you were better off blocking things. With Beata, this was often the case. Not always a brain file, he reminded himself, as she blabbed away, sometimes he had to go into being a solid immovable rock.

Becoming a stone, a rock, was a very important skill. It was related to being bored, another skill. Being bored helped establish his space as well as his superiority. Being still and doing as little as possible took a huge amount of effort. There were times to be a sponge, this skill was important and related to his brain file. But there were times to be a rock. It was an ownership thing. A person needs to own their own space. It was possible—he tried accessing his brain file, but it was hard, as he was so focused on doing nothing—that he'd gotten the owning-your-own-space idea from Stephanie. From Psychology 101. As he lay there on Beata's futon, he felt his manly body, his large male presence, edify into a statue. He was immovable.

"Doughty." Now she gently and slowly, but more aggressively, started touching his shoulder, moving his shoulder, shaking him a bit.

He grunted quietly at first and resisted so that her pushes with her wimpy, skinny arms didn't work. He could not be moved. She stopped. She was next to him on the futon, this he knew without having to open his eyes because his senses, his smell and feel, were acute. Also, he could smell the coffee and it did smell good.

She started pushing him again, but he was a man statue. "Doughty? Doughty, I'm showering." He listened to her pad out of the door again and this time down the hall. Then she came back and presumably did some woman stuff and then got dressed. She was milling about and even though it bothered him, he stayed still. It was exhausting, being so still. It took work.

"Doughty." She pulled the covers down and was being very aggressive. He wanted to slap her bird face, but that sort of violence, he knew, was unwarranted in this moment, and being coolheaded was important at all times. If you were going to use physical means of force, instead of other kinds, it was important to think it through. He did smack her hand away.

"Huh, what?" He sat up. "Ouch!"

"I brought you coffee, it's probably cold by now. You need to get up. It's almost three."

"Baby, baby, *stop*." On yet another milk crate next to the futon was a large book where sat the cold coffee. Her room was littered with neatly piled-up milk crates. He picked up the coffee and looked at it like it was a dead animal and put it back down. He noted the book was about someone named Georgia O'Keeffe.

"Can you bring me a warm coffee?" His voice was pitch-perfect. Demanding, but also bewildered. How dare she? Cold coffee? Really.

She was wearing loose-fitting black jeans over her spaghetti legs, and a loose green T-shirt. Gone was the padded bra, gone was any bra today, and it was just her tiny mounds poking out, the glittery red heart necklace around her throat. She pursed her thin lips and started out of the room.

He wasn't ready to get up. Or look outside yet. He'd see it eventually, her neighborhood, in the light of day. But he decided to pee.

"Where's the bathroom?"

"Just down the hall."

The toilet was clean, but the medicine cabinet was boring. Aspirin, Advil, some deodorant. He moved around some shaving stuff. A roommate's, he suspected.

He was back on the futon under the blanket when she returned with the coffee.

"Here."

Doughty took the coffee. "What is that?" He pointed to some painted things next to the whiteboard things.

"I paint for fun."

He was going to grunt, but instead he did a hard "HA!"

A tiny wave of pain and confusion crossed her face. It was brief. "Listen, thanks so much for taking me home last night, but I have a busy day."

He grunted this time. "Doing what? Painting?" He pointed at the paintings and shook his head, and grunt-laughed. It was a fun combination, the grunt-laugh. He'd invented it himself, just now. Amazing.

"No. I have a five P.M. class at Pace, then I have an eight P.M. shift at Milady's. I was trying to tell you earlier. I'm leaving now and so you need to leave, too." She put her hands on her hips.

Why did women do that? So funny. He laughed.

"Doughty, this isn't funny."

"Baby, baby, *relax*."

"You need to leave with me. My roommates don't know you. I can't leave you here."

He took a long, lovely, calming moment. This, too, he'd gotten from Psychology 101. There was a section on behavioral psychology and something about breathing. "I can get to know them," he said sweetly. This got a smile out of her.

"Not now. I don't have time." She sat on the corner of the bed. "Come on."

"Let me take a quick shower."

Beata conceded and started cleaning things around her room in some manner. No one loved to clean more that Beata. Poor women's gift to the world, cleaning. They loved it. Just loved cleaning.

He took a long, wonderful shower. The bar soap was just Ivory, but the shampoo and conditioner were of a decent quality, not department store stuff like at Sophia's but not generic, either. The water was deliciously hot and the water pressure was stellar. He masturbated slowly, taking his time. His dick was amazing, his chest was muscular. He thought briefly of Sophia, then he thought of Stephanie's huge boobs, then Lew's sister. Then he thought of his cocaine. Then, strangely, his brain landed on the old man's veiny head from Grand Central, which made him soft. Then he gave up. This was okay. He would save his load for another time. This was something that needed to be done from time to time, saving it. His precious liquid.

—

HE WALKED BEATA to the F train. She seemed stressed.

"Aren't you coming with me?"

"No, I have time before my next meeting. I'm going to check out your neighborhood. I'll see you later. At Milady's?"

"Okay, whatever!"

That was rude, Doughty thought.

After she went into the subway, he walked down Smith Street toward Brooklyn Heights and then found his way to the Brooklyn Bridge. He walked over it, then through Chinatown, and turned west to SoHo. It was after 4 p.m. He was getting hungry and he was outside the Mercer. He stood, smoking. He looked up to see if Sophia was home, but there was no movement in her windows. He paced a bit. She must be at her office in Midtown. He started uptown, then decided to double-check the address for Little, Brown. He turned east on Prince Street instead, and walked to a phone booth on Prince and Mott. It was so cozy, with plexiglass walls on all three sides, the big phone book attached to a thick metal coil that attached to the metal phone encasement. He looked up the address.

He was grateful for his stamina but knew that it wasn't just a gift; it was something he had to maintain, too. He then turned uptown and walked fast and focused. He felt all the walking in his legs, felt their strength, felt his power surging through his entire body.

Chapter 12

"Sophia!" She still was wearing those awful clogs, but he liked the business casual look she was sporting. A button-down blouse and a knee-length skirt. She also had on quite a lot of makeup. Blush, lipstick, mascara. Her face resembled the faces of the mothers of many of his Darien friends.

He gave her his most loving, winning smile. He even briefly opened his mouth. He was clean, he had used someone's toothbrush at Beata's, slathered it with super minty Colgate, and sprayed a generous dose of musk-scented deodorant into his armpits. It was not his favorite, but it did the trick.

She looked surprised, her mouth agape, which was wonderful, so he opened his arms and walked toward her to hug her.

"What are you doing here?"

"I came to surprise you!" he said. "You look like you could

use a drink. I know a bar around here that you'll love. It's not Lucy's, but it's got a similar vibe." He had no idea about any of the bars, but he also knew that he would find one. It was NYC.

"You're wearing the same clothes," she said. She was a little stiff under his embrace, but vodka would change that. "You smell clean, though."

He laughed heartily. "I'm a dude! Lazy." Then he did a half laugh, half grunt, and although he wasn't crazy about it, he gave her the sheepish look. Why grown women wanted their men to be boyish, he didn't understand, but 97 percent of the time it was a winning move.

"Let's go?" He looked down at her. He could look down at her, which felt nice. Maybe that was the one redeeming quality of her clogs. Unlike a sexy pair of stilettos, they didn't make her taller. They walked down Broadway and turned west. She had the shakes, but not so bad. Her eyes had that wild look and her body was shivering a bit. She probably couldn't pick up a glass if she had to without using two hands. The sooner he found a place for her, the better. She was pretty quiet. She did prattle a bit about an author. Blablabla. At one point she asked, "Are you listening to me?"

"What are you, a schoolteacher?" He bumped into her, flirtatiously. "Huh? Checking in on me?"

She laughed. She had a pretty face for an old lady. She wasn't a total ruin yet. It was her jawline that was most disturbing. It sagged and had lines. Weirdly her forehead was okay, her eyes were still nice. But he wanted a drink, too. Some beer goggles would help.

He had made her walk west to Eighth Avenue, then they turned downtown and walked past some seedy bars. "Let's just stop," she said. She really was shaky.

"Just one more block, I know a place," he said. They turned onto Fifty-First Street and there was a bar called Posh. What a great name for a bar. It wasn't a total dive bar but it wasn't "posh," either. A gay bar in Midtown. Fantastic. "Here we are! You're going to love it."

They walked in and it wasn't crowded, it was early enough in the afternoon, which was good, but it was no Lucy's. The walls were covered in photos of gay icons and Madonna was playing loudly. It was a little jarring, but the bartender was young and muscular and poured them drinks, a vodka for her, a Maker's and ginger for him. He loved this place. It screamed of cocaine and poppers. Sophia's face, which had been tense and worried, quickly melted into relief as the second round of drinks came fast and large. He really had a tremendous feel for the city and how to find the right place at the right time. After the second round, she was delighted to be there.

They should have waited until rush hour was completely over, but instead she hailed a cab and they fooled around in the back. Why women thought this was fun was beyond him. Especially a woman her age, but after a large part of a bottle of vodka, Sophia didn't know her age, or much else. When they finally got back to her building, he carried her book bag up the steps to her loft for her.

Being helpful was a way of being indispensable. And being indispensable was not hard with Sophia. The woman was a soggy bucket of need. This wasn't luck. This was his mind perfectly attuned to the world around him. He looked down at his arms as he dropped her bag on the floor next to the door when they got inside. They were vibrating with his inner greatness.

Now it was time for the fucking. She slurred something about having him take off her clothes, trying to twirl around, but he didn't do that. He did not undress women. It was important to offer the things he wanted to offer. He had carried her bag upstairs, which on another day, he would not do for her, because he didn't want her getting the wrong idea about him, he didn't work for her. It was important not to do things that he thought were beneath him. She was not a child, she did not need help getting undressed. Well, she was wasted and having trouble getting undressed, but that wasn't his problem. As he watched her struggle, and that confusion thing washed over her face, he stayed firm. Every woman loves a fascist. His father's mantra was now his and it was the best of all the lessons he'd learned from his father. Even better than the grunt.

When he first entered her, it was dry and his dick took a deep turn down. He was banging into something else through her cunt—her intestines? But once he got it in there, balls-deep in there, something gave, and the wetness came. She moaned. He dug in more, getting the wet out. There was always spit but he didn't want to bother if he didn't need to. Dig, dig, downward. The thing about the dryness was the tightness of it, the friction. But he needed to be able to move his dick without it chafing. That perfect balance. Too wet had its issues.

She said, "Let me get some lube," and reached for her side drawer but he swatted her hand away and went at it.

She got loud, which was okay. He stayed focused. Her moans started turning from that fine line of good pain to bad pain, and her wetness was going away, so he realized he needed to finish up.

He pulled out while his dick was still hard and straddled her.

"I'm going to come on your face."

"Come on my face." She opened her mouth.

He stroked himself and finished the job, then lay down next to her.

She got up to pee, moaning.

"Jesus, you're big," she said. "My pussy hurts."

"Sorry. NOT!" he said, proudly.

She gave out a little laugh. They ordered a pizza and something like domestic bliss settled over them that evening. When he went to the bathroom, he pocketed almost all her Xanax, counting fifteen pills and leaving five, and swallowed two. He read the bottle, the prescription was for thirty and the date was almost four months ago. That meant she probably had forgotten about them.

The next morning when she was leaving for work, he did not move.

"Doughty? I'm leaving for work."

He felt her breathing next to him, sitting on the bed. He kept his breath long and slow. "Doughty?"

She began with the pushing and today he was in no mood.

"What, what!? I'm sleeping." He grunted, but he did not open his eyes, and he did not look at her.

"Just close the door behind you, then. It'll lock itself."
He didn't answer. He was, after all, asleep. And sleep he did.

WHEN HE GOT up, it was a little past 3 P.M. He peed, then
went into the kitchen and opened her fridge. Literally almost
nothing. Some old Chinese takeout containers, a box of pizza.
He took out the pizza box. There were two slices left, and he
started to shove a slice in his mouth. There was also a carton of
milk and a bottle of orange juice. He guzzled the juice down
and then went toward the front of her loft and sat at her desk.
Next to it was a filing cabinet with two drawers. The top
drawer had all sorts of manuscripts filed by names of authors.
The bottom drawer was different. He took some files and sat
on the couch. The late-summer sun was streaming in from
Prince Street. He spread out her bank statements. Wow, her
salary was surprisingly low. Forty-five thousand dollars a year.
But every month, there was a deposit of two thousand dollars
from something called a trust account. There was another file
labeled "Trust." She had almost a million dollars, $874,370 to
be exact, in her trust. Not bad. Not bad at all.

Doughty never did anything like treat her loft with respect,
because he was a man and being neat and careful didn't leave
much for her to do and women needed to clean and tidy up,
even if they had help, which Sophia did have. Once a week,
she told him, a woman came and cleaned. He had yet to meet
this woman, but anyway, being a slob was being a man. But
here, here he had found out something very important. So
with utmost care, with a gentle and deliberate touch he hadn't
known was in him, he very carefully put the files back exactly

as he had found them. He even thought of dusting the cabinet. He had such control, thanks to Mr. Miyagi, thanks to himself, thanks to his knowledge of when and where to be what he needed to be. He remembered the exact width of each file, how they'd been spaced, where they'd touched, as he put them back. But before he did that, he wrote down the account numbers, and the amounts in the tiniest of handwriting, in the back of his phone book. He could barely read it himself. And he wrote her full name and birth date, too. Sophia Elizabeth Bowen. Then he went back to bed and, lulled by a peaceful buzz of accomplishment, fell asleep.

WHEN SHE GOT home that evening, he was showered and was watching the news in the living room, eating the last slice of pizza. He'd had a good day. As Sophia entered the loft, he heard her drop her keys in the kitchen and then she came into the living room.

"You're still here."

"I am."

"You didn't go to work?"

"I did not. I took some calls. I used your phone. I hope you don't mind." He did not look at her because he was watching the news. The news would help him. It was important to know what was going on in the world. The news was grim. The economy was bad. Clinton, a white-trash embarrassment to the United States, had replaced Bush last year. What a stupid liberal redneck, a disgrace. He missed Bush. Bush was a Yale man. So he didn't know things, like that they spoke German in Austria, but who cared? He came from a nice family, and didn't pander to the socialists in the country. He was all about small government. And was financially conservative. Clinton was a clown.

"That's fine," she said from the kitchen, where he heard her get the vodka out of the freezer and pour herself a drink.

Now she was standing between him and the television.

"Hey, you're in the way," he said. "I'm watching the news."

"Okay," she said. She seemed contrite. Good. She sat next to him. But he was a stone.

"Move over a bit," he said. He looked at her straight in the face, she was sitting so close to him he could smell her perfume, even her breath. She was wearing a shirtdress, with a brown leather belt around the waist. He did not smile. "You're crowding me."

"What?"

"Move." He gave her a push. Not hard. Not soft.

She moved over a bit. She sipped her drink.

"Just kidding. Here," he said, and patted the couch next to him. She was perfectly confused. It made life exciting. It made him mysterious and unpredictable. She came closer to him. He put an arm around her.

"The news is depressing," she said, sipping away.

"Stop it!" he said, loudly. He kept his arm on her. She seemed alarmed, but the right amount of alarmed. She tried to pull away, but he tightened his arm on her. Her expression, which he saw out of his side-eye, was somewhere between disbelief and confusion. Somewhere between "Is he kidding?" and "Is this for real?" He stared at the TV. Blabla. The economy. Blabla. "Let me watch, for God's sake." Doughty said.

She said nothing. The quiet was exactly right.

Every woman loves a fascist.

LATER, AFTER SHE'D had just enough vodka to be back to normal but not enough to be sloppy, they went to Fanelli's on Prince Street, where she bought them a perfectly mediocre dinner. He looked out the window, wondering if he would see Beata on her way to Milady's, just a little farther west on Prince Street. Then they went back up to her place and started the fucking again. He pulled out at one point. Her pussy was warm and wet, and he went down on her.

This was nice. He liked the control, obviously, and his method was similar to the patience he used to achieve his stillness, his rock-solidness. He stayed there, his tongue wet and flat, his mouth moving up and down, side to side, round and round a bit, changing pressure, his head shaking like a wet dog on occasion. Waiting, and loosely gripping her legs. Then he let go of her leg with his left hand and put a finger in her cunt. He took his finger out, all wet, and put it in her ass and—boom—she came. He pulled away to look at her. She was writhing. He watched her, slightly bored, his dick on medium. Then he got on her and finished himself off inside her while her body was as loose as a dead person from her orgasm, her brain shut off completely.

So this was how it was. Now the questions would stop. This would be the only thing she needed from him. The next morning, when she left and he was immovable, she said, "I left you a key. It's next to you, on the side table." He did not respond, as he was asleep, but after that, he came and went as he pleased.

Chapter 13

So it went. The summer ended and it was fall. He would mostly stay at Sophia's, and on the rare occasion he stayed with Beata, she wasn't as grateful for his presence as he would've liked. He told Sophia he had rented a place with his high school friends in the West Village and she was delighted for him. She needed him, he knew it, and she did, too, although every now and then he had to really make it clear to her that he was the best thing that had happened to her in a long time.

"Whatever happened to the house you were buying? You must be sick of your roommates, not that you stay there much."

"I'm in the process of selling it. We're closing tomorrow," he said.

Sophia, with her glasses on, was sitting at her desk with a book she was editing. She needed a shower. Her lips were colorless and seemed dry. She looked up at him. "What? That's so great, Doughty!"

"Do you want me to get your purse? You could use some

lipstick." Before she answered, he'd gotten up and retrieved her purse. "Here," he said, and thrust it at her.

She stood for a hug and he let her hug him.

"We should celebrate," she said. "Also, I'd love to meet your friends. I'll take you all out."

He ignored her. And walked to the shower. When he came back, her face was back in the manuscript. He went to the door and said, "I have to run."

"Wait, Doughty?" But he slammed the door and left. He loved slamming her door. A large, heavy industrial door, the weight of it making the sound so thorough. SLAM.

BEATA WORKED THREE nights at Milady's and had left the Cherry Tavern altogether. The Wops who ran Milady's had moved her into the apartment on Mulberry Street, as she'd hoped. He stayed alert to the possibility of running into her, or running into Sophia when he, not so frequently, was with Beata. Weirdly, he did not fuck Beata. They snuggled like "friends." Still, it was important to have this option, especially now that she was out of Brooklyn, thank God, despite the loft being a better fit for his current needs. And even though he hadn't run into one when with the other, he thought it was probably just a matter of time, and he played out variations on how he'd handle it. He looked forward to the challenge, and he enjoyed mentally workshopping strategies for managing the two women. For instance, if he were with Beata and were to run into Sophia. "Beata," he would say, "this is my colleague Sophia! She sends clients my way, friends who are looking to buy or sell." Sophia would be confused and need a drink. Later, he'd explain to her that she had said she'd send people his way. She'd be ashamed that she didn't remember, and would pretend that she did, but she was blacked out so much that she'd believe it. Or then, the more likely one, where he would be with Sophia, because he was with her more often by far. He would walk right by Beata, and say "I don't know that woman" if Beata tried to say anything to him. That was his favorite scenario. Later, he'd apologize to Beata and explain he'd been with a very difficult client. Playing out the scenarios was good mental practice. He was always pushing his mind and body practices. The vigorousness of these practices paid off. He felt it, this robust mind-body health, felt it flow in the blood that went through his limbs and torso and dick and gently but strongly pulsed in his brain organ.

Beata's new place in Little Italy was a 375-square-foot railroad apartment on the first floor, whose front and only windows looked out on the building's garbage cans. Yet it was a step up from Brooklyn, to say the least. It was safe. What really bothered him was that she presumed she was doing him a favor by letting him stay there. This made his blood pressure rise when he thought about it, so he had methods to alleviate this discomfort. It wasn't easy, but when he managed to engage her in conversation, it always helped. Also, he reminded her regularly how he'd helped her move. Eventually, she'd gotten prickly about this reminder. And the thing was, it made him double down on the reminding. Until her prickliness went away, until she just got sick of arguing. This was related to being a rock. Never stop being right when you are right. Repetition was important, like practicing karate. Never back down. Winning was not negotiable; he would win, he wouldn't stop a conversation until he won it. Win or die. This was what made him the man he was.

"I know you helped Joe move me. I am grateful. But sometimes, I need to be alone to do my homework. I have work to do. You need to leave so I can concentrate." She said this to him while he was resting on her futon.

Joe Bird, her friend from Milady's, was a small problem. He had a van, and yes, he'd done the lifting during the move, all of it in fact. Doughty didn't want to get the new shirts Sophia had bought him dirty, plus he just didn't like lifting things. Joe was a strange, large man who could lift a desk with one hand. Doughty had watched the van. The van had needed watching. At the end of the afternoon, Joe didn't shake his hand. But Doughty forgave him. "Glad I could help out, Joe." He then put his arm around Beata. It was slightly awkward. "Oh and, Joe, I have two friends who are moving to NYC soon. I can ask them to hire you."

Joe looked at him with his shiny blue eyes in his red, beer-drinking face and laughed. "No can do, Dotty. I'm doing this as a favor to Bee." Doughty, for the first time, noticed that Joe's thick hair was gray. Was it premature? How old was he? It didn't matter, so he erased that thought from his mind.

But it was true, Stan and Lew were moving to the city in the fall. Joe was too stupid to understand he was passing up a good opportunity to make some cash. At least Doughty had tried.

"I leave you alone a lot," Doughty said. "I need to finish watching this show. Just leave *me* alone for a little bit. I'm not asking much. Please. Just be quiet. I'm being quiet." Beata was sitting at her pathetic kitchen table, clearly made from plywood, which served as a desk for her. "We go so far back. We have *history*. I love seeing you. It's important we see each other." Stating this truth, repeatedly, helped ingrain it into Beata's being. It was a technique similar to ones used by Tony Robbins, whose book *Unlimited Power* his father had owned. Because, for one, it was true. And truth matters. You can take a truth and do so much with it. She was fortunate to know him, a young man from a nice town, a nice family, with a community of ambitious people from his world who were really going somewhere, of which she was not part. Regardless, he found it charming to watch Beata forge her way in New York. Sitting there with her books, he'd roll around in his mind all the things she had against her: her lowly background, her hard-working, ignorant unworldliness, her small breasts, her working-class accent and this clothing thing—what was it? Grunge?

Her television wasn't as nice as Sophia's—it was smaller and she didn't have a VCR, and she had rabbit ears on her TV, no cable, whereas Sophia had premium cable—but it was important to be with her. She needed him, and he needed to remind her she did, so he'd forgive her bad television. After a couple of hours of that, after she got up and made two turkey sandwiches for them, and brought him one to where he was, she returned to her homework.

"What on God's earth are you studying now?" He got up. He was bored. He walked over to her and tapped on her large textbook. He felt like her professor.

"I'm taking an elective on psychology."

"That was my major at Boston College," he said.

"I thought you studied economics?"

"I did. I had a double major."

"Aren't you going to the office today?"

It was a Saturday. "I have the weekend off."

She looked up from her book and he sat next to her in the only other chair at her tiny kitchen table. It was sad, she didn't even have room for a proper desk. But he forgave that. So much forgiving of Beata. It was part of being her fascist. After enforcing the control, you then needed to do all this forgiving. He leaned over and shut the book.

"Hey," she said.

"What?" He had her attention.

"I thought Saturday was a busy day for real estate?"

"It is if you're in a lowly position, hustling to rent apartments all day." He had finished his sandwich and left the plate next to her books, standing up. "I'm way past that."

"Oh," she said. She wasn't listening.

The day turned into afternoon, which turned into evening. She'd left and come back. He forgot why. Then the time came for her to go to work.

"Doughty, I've got a shift at eight P.M. You need to leave."

"Just make me a key. Then we won't have this problem anymore."

"I'm not sure I want to do that."

"It will make things easier for when I need to be downtown for work. I help you all the time. In fact, I can make the key for you. You need to have some spares. What if you got locked out? Let me help you."

"I want to come see your place uptown sometime," she

said. "But I was thinking of making a key to leave at the bar just in case. I guess you could make one for yourself."

"Just give me forty dollars and I'll have it done tomorrow while you sleep in. Leave me your key. So you can sleep in tomorrow."

"Forty bucks? Are you serious?"

"Beata! Of course it's forty bucks! You're going to be late!" He put his hand out. "Give them to me. Give me two twenties, I'll get some copies made. You need them!"

"Okay, okay, but bring me change because there is no way it's forty bucks. I gotta go."

THE WEEKS PASSED and the holidays were approaching. He had keys to Sophia's and Beata's and all was going well. Was it hard to manage these two apartments? Yes. But he was young, virile, and powerful. It was part of a longer-term plan, being there for these two needy women. He slept a lot, he walked a lot, and learned a lot from the televisions, but he missed his encyclopedias. He missed learning more about history. Current affairs and facts were important, but he wanted all the knowledge at his fingertips. It was time to retrieve his library.

Chapter 14

Thanksgiving came and he went back to Darien. Prior to his return to his hometown, he had rented a storage place in Brooklyn, where storage was cheap, even though at that time he hadn't put anything in it. As disgusting as the times he had spent in Beata's apartment there were, he'd used them to his benefit. Poor neighborhoods had their use, so once, he had walked around the quiet neighborhood after she'd left for work, taking in the large low-income government-housing projects just blocks from Beata's pathetic room, which led him to a large storage facility on Third Avenue. He rented a 250-square-foot storage unit for forty dollars a month. He signed a three-month lease.

Thanksgiving had its ups and downs. His mother was doing well, which made her more difficult to be around. In fact, since moving into Mrs. Hutton's apartment over the flower shop, she seemed healthier, more alert, when he occasionally called her. But now, here he was in Darien, above a flower shop, back on the couch he'd crashed on when his father died.

It wasn't a bad couch, but it wasn't a room to himself, which men like him needed and deserved.

He came up the Saturday before the long weekend so he could help his mother. He was a dutiful son, and even though he needed to forge his own way in the world, he never forgot her. Lew and Stan, who'd moved to the city that September, took the train on Wednesday night before Thanksgiving, so it wasn't until the night after the holiday dinner that they got together. They decided that Doughty would pick them up and they'd drive to Midway for old times' sake.

Doughty stole a bottle of Jack Daniel's from his mother. She was in front of the little TV and drinking, but she'd been drinking less and the kitchen was just a part of the main room, where he was sleeping and where she was watching TV in her same indestructible turquoise snap-button house robe.

"What are you looking for?"

"Mom, just watch your show. I'm going out."

She stood, revealing her vein-riddled naked calves, so appalling his jaw almost dropped, her feet in what were once white slippers that now were brown all along the edges.

"Sit down, Mom. I know Dad's not here to be the king of the castle, but when I'm here, I'm the king of the castle, got it?"

He was bent over, opening cabinets, and found the bottles. He looked at her, standing there, an abomination to the eyes, a thing one looks away from. "Mom, I said sit down. You're ruining my concentration."

She sat. "I just was going to help you. I hated it when your father said that, by the way."

He had the bottle in his backpack. He walked over to her. "You needed him. Now you have me. Every woman needs a fascist, remember that one?"

She was wearing her stubborn face, and he could tell she didn't like that one, either. He didn't have time for yelling. He sighed. "Bye, Mom."

"When are you coming home?"

"Late." He was half out the door, the spare keys she'd given him in his hand.

"Will you take me out to the diner tomorrow?"

"Yes," he lied.

"I'm so proud of you, Doughty," she said, and he shut the door.

IT WASN'T SO cold for November, but it wasn't warm. No one had gloves on. There they all were, in his mother's car.

"To Doughty," Lew said, and took a huge swig from the bottle. "The designated driver."

"And booze provider," said Stan, grabbing the bottle.

Sitting on the rocks in Midway, Doughty lit a joint and passed it around. He watched contently as his friends got fucked up. He watched as their eyes got swimmy, their voices got louder, and all the things started just coming out of their mouths. Who they'd fucked, how shitty their dads were, how much they loved NYC, how hard Wall Street was, how shitty being a gopher was. How much money they were making.

The moneymaking talk got intense. It involved getting physical as it was the most emotional thing for his friends. There was some wrestling even, and Stan got pushed hard

down from his rock perch and cut his forehead on another
rock. It was a small cut but there was blood. Alcohol thinned
the blood so it was flowing more than it would otherwise.
Doughty filed away the exact amounts of money they were
making, something they never would have said sober. Lew
was making ten grand more a year than Stan, and Stan was
making sixty grand a year. Their rent was sixteen hundred dollars a month, which they split in half. Stan got angry, Lew was
making more money and paying the same rent, even though
he was in the bigger bedroom. And wiping the blood from
his cut with his sweatshirt pissed him off, too. Not that it was
surprising to him, the extra ten G's Lew made. He was a Jew,
even though he and his family lied about it. Alcohol increased
testosterone. Hence, drunk fights. It was not as if aggression
weren't a part of young men, but Doughty loved watching the
loss of control, the extra desire for violence alcohol brought to
the human body. Ignition. Doughty poured a small amount
of the whiskey on some leaves and lit them. A small fire tried
to come to life. Doughty blew on it, waved a hand over it,
watching the flames rise and the leaves burn.

"I should be paying less! My room is smaller! You have the
bigger room, you fucking faggot!" Stan yelled. There wasn't a
lot of ground in the pathway of Midway, but there they were
again, in the dirt. "Jewing me over the rent!"

Lew tried to punch him and Stanny grabbed his arm. The
fire Doughty started was growing and he snatched at more
leaves with both hands and threw them on the flame. It spiked
higher and Stan and Lew saw it and backed off and sat on
their respective rock seats.

"What the fuck!" Stanny said, wiping the dripping wound on his head.

Lew laughed. "Doughty, what the hell."

"Relax, pussies." Doughty began stomping the fire out. It took a minute. But it sobered them up.

The drive home was quiet. The roads were lightly lit and empty. They passed one cop car. Stanny had balled up his sweatshirt and was pressing it against his wound. The bleeding stopped. Doughty dropped off Stanny first. Lew, who had been asleep, woke up. Doughty drove up near to Lew's house, and parked a good distance away, so one could see it in all its manor-like splendor. He turned off the lights.

"Take me up the driveway, you dick," Lew said.

"Get out of my car."

"Your mother's car."

Doughty wanted to punch him. But Lew was too sobered up. He sat silently, looking toward Lew's house.

"You afraid? What are you afraid of?" Lew leaned forward from the back seat, his face right next to Doughty's ear. "My family hates you. Fucking disgrace to this town. Even though the sign on your lawn has a broker's name on it, everyone knows the bank owns it. And no one has bought it yet because it's a falling down, piece-of-shit house."

Doughty said nothing. He lit a cigarette, cracked open the window. "Eat my dick, Lew the Jew."

"Later, dude." And out he went. Lew had gotten broader. He kept getting broader. He watched his friend walk down the road and then turn right up his long driveway.

Doughty smoked three more cigarettes. He picked up the

nearly empty bottle of Jack from the floor of the passenger seat. There was just the right amount left. He swigged. He looked at his watch. It was now 1 A.M. He'd been sitting there for forty-five minutes. He got out.

ALL THE TREES, all that expensive landscaping, made it easy to walk in the dark around the perimeter of the house. The house was one of the few and most well-known modern builds in Darien. It had windows that were so large they exhibited the entire interior to the outdoors. There were floodlights around the house mostly situated in the front- and back-door areas. Even so, they didn't penetrate the trees. He walked through them until he had a great angle of Lew's sister Kristen's room. Then, finding the shadows, he walked along the manicured lawn toward her window. When he got close enough to it, he lay down in the dark on the grass, half hidden by a bush, propping his upper torso up on his elbows. A bedside light was on in her room. She had the curtains pulled almost shut, but there was a large enough vertical opening on one end of the window so he could see in through the long length of it. Her desk, her bed, the silhouette of her body. She got up and left and turned on the hallway light. Probably went to the bathroom. He was hard.

She came back and his eyes had adjusted to the dimness, the way the shades made everything into shapes. She turned off the light and got in bed wearing men's boxer shorts and a tank top. What was this wearing-clothing-to-bed thing? Did they hate their bodies so much they couldn't even be naked when they were alone? Maybe they were afraid. That almost made him laugh out loud. Women. He pulled his pants down to his knees, and leaning on his right side, began stroking himself. He stood, stooping, and with his pants around his ankles, shuffled to the window. He breathed on it and there was his mark, a wet cloud on the pristine window. He came on some bushes and went home.

LEW AND STAN were taking the train on Sunday, but he waited until the following Thursday to return. His mother would work downstairs at the flower shop, he'd relax, eat all her food, and watch TV and masturbate. It was a real vacation and he was glad he could be there for his mother as well.

"Don't you need to get back to work, Bobby?" his mother asked. After working in the flower shop that day, she had grocery shopped. She was carrying a bag of groceries and a bag with a large bottle of whiskey. As the week passed, she was drinking more.

"It's a really slow time for real estate, Mom, you have to know that. It doesn't take incredible intelligence to understand that people are not buying apartments and houses during the holiday season. This is just common sense, Ma. You don't need a degree in business to know something as banal as that."

"Okay, I'm sorry, Bobby." She started unpacking the food and the booze. She apologized all the time. His father had trained her well. Funny, at the beginning of the week she'd been less apologetic, but he'd gotten her back in shape.

He was stretched out on the couch. He was rereading the entry on condensation in the encyclopedia. A really nice thing about being home was having his *Encyclopedia Britannica*s, which thankfully his stupid mother had not thrown out. "Condensation usually refers to the change of water from the gas phase into the liquid phase, and is the reverse of vaporization. It can also be considered as the change in the state of water vapor to liquid water when it makes contact with a liquid or solid surface. When this transition happens from the gaseous phase into the solid phase, the change is called deposition."

He'd been jerking off all week to that fog on the window, his condensation on her window. Kristen asleep in her dumb man underwear, huddling in fear on her bed. He shut the book and sat up.

"I bought some TV dinners for old times' sake. And I bought you beer, too." She had a drink and gave him an open beer and sat in the same little blue armchair she'd brought from their old house. "Maybe we can watch a game show." She was wearing glorified sweatpants and a matching sweatshirt.

After a little bit, she asked, "What were you reading about?"

"I was reading about the biology of condensation."

"That's strange." She sipped and half smiled.

"No, Mom, it's not strange. The sciences are not strange. Did you know that liquid turning into solid is called 'deposition'? Did you know that 'deposition' is also a legal term that lawyers use when they get information from a person for a trial? Do you know how steam is made? Did you know that the water cycle is one of the reasons there is human life on this planet? Is it *strange* to want to know how we got here? Some people have more knowledge than 'That's a pretty flower,'

Mom. Not everyone has nothing to talk about, or to offer to a conversation."

She was halfway through her first drink. He looked at her. She looked very old. "I'm sorry, Bobby." It didn't sound sincere and he noted that. Then she started up again.

"I've actually learned a lot about the different kinds of flowers, the difference between perennials and annuals . . ."

"Oh my God, Mom, shut up. I'm not in kindergarten anymore."

"Sorry, Bobby."

THE NEXT DAY, when she came back from work, before she took him to the train station, Doughty asked, "How much do you get paid to work at the flower shop?"

She was wearing blue jeans. She stood with her back to him, pouring herself a drink. He had left her a pile of dishes in the sink.

"Jesus, Mom, blue jeans. What are you, a teenager? How embarrassing."

"Emily says they look nice."

"Emily is retarded. Also her name is Mrs. Hutton, not Emily."

"I call her Emily, Bobby."

"I don't call her Emily, Mom. So don't call her Emily when you talk to me about her, Mom."

"Okay, I'm sorry."

"It's Mrs. Hutton, Mom."

"Okay, Bobby, Mrs. Hutton says . . ."

"I don't care what Mrs. Hutton says about your stupid blue jeans."

"Okay, I'm sorry."

"Stop saying you're sorry."

This was his favorite part. He watched her open her mouth. She was going to say sorry. Sorry for saying sorry. It was theater. Then she shut her mouth.

"How much does Mrs. Hutton pay you?"

She took a long sip. She didn't like the question. But she knew she had to say. Otherwise, there would be a lot of sorry-saying. "Bobby."

"Do you get paid in cash?"

Chapter 15

He took the A train straight from Grand Central to his storage space in Brooklyn. It was so nice that it was open 24/7. He turned on the garish overhead, and started unpacking the large suitcase he'd taken from his mother's place and made neat piles of his stuff. He carefully moved all the solid objects he had—to start with, the first five volumes of the 1974 *Encyclopedia Britannica*, as well as a medical textbook, his dictionary and thesaurus, and Stephanie's Psych 101 textbook. He had left some stuff at his mother's apartment—his VCR and his videos, his toolbox. He'd pick them up at Christmas. It was all good. Then, with the joy of a child knocking down a train set he'd just built, he threw all the clothes he'd brought, mostly warm sweaters and his L.L.Bean puffer jacket, all newly washed in Mrs. Hutton's laundry room off of her main house, and the one set of sheets he'd taken from his mother's closet, into a messy pile and turned off the overhead light and lay down. It was nice enough. He was tired. He fell into his deep, dark sleep.

The next day, he woke and looked at his watch. It was 8 A.M. There was noise outside his unit. He listened. The only sound he heard was that of one person in the hall, and the dull swish of a mop. He didn't hear keys jangle. He didn't hear voices. He needed to pee, so he grabbed an empty tall boy he'd brought just for this occasion, and carefully putting his dick right next to the sharp opening, released a heavy stream. When he saw that the can was filling up, he moved to the corner of the storage space, put the can down, and watched it almost overflow. He squeezed his dick muscles, shutting off any dribble. Why hadn't he taken a roll of paper towels just in case? So many things to do and think about. Then he went back to his sleep mound and shut his eyes and went back to sleep.

At 4 P.M. there was a shift change. He heard voices. Then silence. He stood and stretched, put on his backpack, locked up behind himself, and left. Walking past a young woman at the desk, he waved, and exited onto the street. It was a beautiful afternoon. The weather had turned to winter, and he jutted his chest out in his navy down jacket, and headed into the city, the city that never sleeps, to call on Sophia. She had missed him, no doubt.

Chapter 16

When he arrived at Sophia's, she was happy to see him and was more of a mess than ever. This was good news. But it wasn't without its challenges. Although he relished his role of caretaker, and she was smart enough to know she owed him greatly for all his help, he still occasionally got tired of her neediness. She did make it to work most days, but she'd had more than a few sick days as time went by, which was annoying. A man needed time to himself. Sometimes, she would stay in her bedroom for most of those days, so he watched television, smoked on the balcony in the cold, and opened the door for the takeout delivery people. Sometimes, she had the gall to ask him to get food and vodka, and to say he should keep the change that he deserved would be an understatement. He knew his worth. He had, as the weeks flew by, managed to save over four hundred dollars for himself. Sophia's dad had died suddenly, and her mother was in Vermont. She had a sister who was flying east from LA to join them in Vermont for Christmas. She had a deadline editing a book. Blablabla. She was leaving for Vermont on the evening of the twenty-third to join them.

The evening she was due to leave, she came to Doughty where he sat on her couch watching the news.

"Doughty," she said, dropping her heavy book bag, and kicking off the clogs. "Let's go to Lucy's when I get back. We haven't gone out in ages. I miss Lucy. She's a downtown icon. I miss that bar, the bar where we met. We never go out anymore."

He shushed her. The TV was on and he was watching it. But this was true. Mostly it was because of her coming. And being sick. Now that he'd made her come, it was all she wanted to do—hang out at her place and get her pussy eaten. He didn't want to go to Lucy's, out of principle, but not because he didn't like the bar. Mostly, it was important to insist on doing what *he* wanted to do. He watched her, her limbs all jangly, coming to sit next to him on the couch, a drink in hand.

Doughty wasn't surprised that Sophia had become so attached to him. It was what was owed to him. His entitlement. He liked her pussy, he liked sucking on her clit, he liked shoving his fingers in her, he liked sticking his dick in her. Her tits were all right. He enjoyed it, but it was work of a kind, so she owed him. She owed him everything, as far as he was concerned. He was a gift to her. He didn't owe her *anything*. It hadn't taken long at all to get into a rhythm. She would get up and get her own drinks. He didn't fetch for her. She would do all the dishes. The few times they went out, he noticed people's eyes on him. This was okay, but he kept an eye on who kept an eye on him. None of them mattered. But it became something to monitor because they always went to the same places near her loft, mostly Fanelli's, as she got lazier and just wanted to fuck.

And then there was the fact that she also was getting sick a lot.

"I think it's the holidays," she said. She had just vomited again. She was throwing up every morning before she had her first vodka. It was gross. He just ignored it and watched the news. "I think I'm anxious about seeing my family. And my dad. My dad is gone."

Oh no, she was about to cry. The first two or three times she had done this, he'd patted her on the back a few times, then fucked her. But now it was getting old. It had been old for over a week.

"You're fine," he said. He was annoyed. It was tiresome to console her, so he mostly didn't anymore. Comforting her went onto his list of things to stop doing. He wasn't her caregiver. People think you work for them, but Doughty didn't work for her. "Just have another drink."

Here was the thing: once you showed kindness, the desire for it just grew and grew. It was human nature, a part that needed to be nipped in the bud, this thing where the person— in this case, Sophia—started to ask for more and more, if you gave in. His father had taught him: "Kindness is a sign of weakness, son." This was part of how you remained king of your castle. By not being weak, for one.

"I don't feel fine."

"Baby, baby, *stop*." He was stretched on the couch. "This couch sucks."

She was sunk into her blue chair. "I keep throwing up."

"*Stop.*" He leaned up and looked straight at her, a hard look. It worked. "You need a new couch. You need a sectional. This one is ugly and has no support anymore." He leaned back again.

"I know. It's old." She was calming down. Distracting her was the best.

"When? When are you going to get a new couch?"

"Not today. I'm leaving for Vermont . . ."

"It's the holidays. It's the holidays. It's the holidays!" Doughty sat up and threw his hand in the air. "So are you going to do it when you get back?" He moved around uncomfortably. "Look at me! I can't get comfortable." Her face was morphing a bit, from "poor me" to irritation. One would think this was a bad thing, but life also was a tightrope, and like any balancing act, he had to push her in various directions. Balance. Putting her in her place meant he had to keep changing that place. Keep her on her toes, balancing, as the rope tremored underneath her.

"Jesus, Doughty." She went pale. She got up and ran to the bathroom and he heard her retch.

When she came back, a fresh vodka in her hand, he glared at her.

He turned back to the TV. "Can you close the door when you do that? It's a huge turnoff to hear you do that."

She sat in her chair and drank. She seemed better. "I think I need you to leave while I pack. I'm really stressed out. Aren't you going home? Don't you need to pack or anything?"

Okay. He'd give her a carrot. "You look better!"

"I feel better. I think it's nerves."

"Of course it is." He focused on the news. A celebrity had died.

"Anyway," she began.

"Don't say 'anyway.' Just say what you want to say. You're not in high school." His eyes remained glued on the television.

The drink was making her a bit confident. She was in that place—the after-she-felt-bad-and-needed-a-drink-but-before-she-was-a-mess place.

"Doughty, I said I want you to leave. Whenever I say this, you ignore me. I love having you here, but sometimes I need the place to myself. Don't you have to get ready to go? Or have some last-minute work before you go visit your mother?" Then she puffed herself up. She stood. There she was, in her god-forsaken clogs, a light blue caftan hiding her bloated stomach, but she was holding her head high. "After the holidays, I want to visit you at work. I want to see your office. You know where I live and work, and I never have seen either where you live or work."

He was going to glare at her, explain, as he had before, how his work was really in the field. That he wasn't going to walk her around. That he had clients. That he was too busy to bring her along anywhere. He continued to watch the news. It was fascinating. Bad things were happening.

"Doughty?"

He felt his inner rock solidify. He felt totally focused. People were upset about the world. It was the news.

"Doughty!" She got up and went into her room. Then she

showered. He heard her pack. When she came out, she was ready to go. "I have a flight to catch. I like getting there early. I like airport bars, you know that."

"I'll lock up after you leave."

"Doughty! Please. Get out!" She was laughing a bit. "Seriously."

"Sophia. You know there are problems right now, all sorts of crises, right? Please. And Jesus, there is stuff going on in Europe and South America." He put a hand up, in her direction. A "stop" hand.

"I don't care about that. I need you to leave."

"What's wrong with you? You don't care about current events of enormous proportions? You don't care about the future of the world?"

"Doughty, I have to go. This is too much. It's not that I don't care about the news, I just . . ."

"You just said you don't care. And you're the one in a hurry, not me."

"Oh my God, I'm leaving. We will talk about this more when I come back." She was upset but she didn't have time to be more demanding, so he took the win. She went to her room, rustling around in there, then to the kitchen to get a drink, then to the bathroom from where he heard more retching, then back to her room.

Then there she was, looking like she pretty much had her shit together, her face powdered, some lipstick on, standing at the door. As she unlocked the door, he got up and walked toward her. The look she gave him! It was funny. She looked so serious. He smiled. He couldn't help himself.

"When I come back, we need to have a serious talk about this situation."

His shoulders went loose and his eyes searched. "Baby." He put his hand gently on her waist and nuzzled her neck. She leaned her crotch on his hip. "I'm going to miss you."

"Call me," she said, and shut the door. "You have my number in Vermont, right?"

"Yes, I do. Oh, I'm going to miss you." He pushed against her, and she pushed back and nuzzled his neck.

"We need to talk about this arrangement. It's not working for me." And she let herself out.

Chapter 17

Finally! He flopped himself onto the couch. He needed some alone time. The last few weeks had been too much. His body tingled with possibility. Christmas was two days from now, he had the place to himself. He called Beata. She didn't pick up. Maybe she was back in Waterbury. He was bored, not in his strategic way, not in his useful way, but in the other way. The way of needing to do something. This was rare. He got up, showered luxuriously slowly, masturbated, and decided to go out and see if Beata was maybe working.

One of the many good things about the city he'd chosen to live in was that even during the holidays, the bars did not close. New York, the city that never sleeps.

He looked at himself in the mirror while brushing his teeth. Soon, he would hint to Sophia about getting his tooth fixed. Not yet. Soon. He turned his face to the left, then the right. His right side was his better profile. He instinctively knew this, as he usually made people sit to the right of him. But it was important to check both sides. Left, then right. Honestly,

both sides were pretty great. He'd really grown into understanding that being fair-haired was nothing to be ashamed of,
particularly his locks, which added a bit of boyishness to his
hard masculinity. The whimsy of his hair contrasted nicely
with his chiseled self. He was chiseled all over. He shook his
hair and ran his fingers through it. The innocent light locks
made him approachable. Very approachable. He felt himself
getting hard again. He smacked his dick a bit, just hitting it
with his palm over his jeans, smack, smack. Then got bored.
He put on his puffer and let himself out.

The streets were beautifully quiet and cold, the sky dark, as
he sauntered down Prince Street. And as luck would have it—
even though he knew his life was not lucky; he made things in
his life line up, his planning and his power and his knowledge
paved his way—he opened the door to Milady's and there was
Beata, behind the bar.

As he entered, he saw through his side-eye a handful of
regulars sitting in the low-lit bar and he opened his arms
toward her and said "Beata!" Then he pulled out a stool and
sat away from the regulars. Despite the weather, she wore a
tight emerald-green sleeveless shirt and had a red ribbon in
her hair.

"Look at you, all festive!"

Joe Bird was there, at the other end of the bar with the
others. Did that guy have nothing better to do? Joe was staring
at him. So uncouth. So low-class. Doughty felt sorry for him,
so he nodded in his direction without looking at him. "Hey,
man."

Nothing. Just the stare. What a moron.

Beata had her arms deep in the sinks, washing glasses. He was used to her black choppy hair by now, but often in his mind, when she was just a thing in his mind, when he jerked off to the vision of her mouth, she still had her fine blond hair, and her rhinestone red necklace dangling around her throat and she choked on his dick.

"Hey, Doughty," she said.

"I'll take a beer."

She pulled one out of the ice. "That's three bucks."

He looked at her. He contemplated a grunt with a quick laugh. He decided not to grunt. "Ha! What's your problem?"

"That's how much a beer costs."

He took out three singles and laid them on the bar. "Is your boss on you?"

"No, it's just that you never pay or tip and it's annoying."

"Babe, why aren't you home?"

"I'm working Christmas. I get paid double time at the hospital. It's fine."

"What hospital?"

"I told you I got a job at Mount Sinai."

He'd forgotten. His brain file didn't have time for all her nonsense. "Let's do shots."

"I have to work tomorrow at the hospital. I am closing early tonight. At midnight."

There it was—an opening. She was lonely. He wasn't going to sit there and talk to her regulars. "I have to go see someone, but I'll come pick you up when you're closing."

Her face got hard.

"Come on, we'll keep each other company." He watched

her soften a bit. Sometimes people needed reminding that
they were all alone in the world and he was there to help with
that.

"Okay."

BOOM. HE WALKED outside, lit a cigarette, and walked
west, all the way west, to the river. He found a bench and sat
there smoking. It was dark and very cold and he liked it. The
highway was pretty quiet. If he walked a few blocks uptown,
things would get interesting. He walked past the dilapidated
buildings facing the highway that were mostly dark, with the
occasional window showing a sad, yellow-lighted interior.
When he got to Christopher Street and the empty, abandoned
docks along the Hudson River, the shadowy scavengers could
be seen in dark corners or walking toward alleys. It was not a
busy night, because it was winter. The cold air invigorated him.
He made out four men in the dark. The twitchier one was his
favorite so he sauntered up. The bargaining was brief. He sat
on a hard plank of wood and smoked a rock the twitchy guy
had given him. He had never smoked crack! It was *amazing*.
WAY more fun than snorting cocaine. Everything great about
Doughty became greater. His mind, his powers, his hair, his
future, his plans. He had the best plans! Anything he planned
was the best plan! He would buy an island after selling all the
undervalued houses in the West Village! He would get Sophia
to fix his tooth and then with his gorgeous new mouth he'd
eat all the pussies and fuck all the models!

The guy gave him twenty bucks. And another rock! Well,
he'd asked if he had one. He smoked it up, while the man

was working his shaft up and down and up and down again. The man looked wealthy, despite the crack, despite the pier blow job. His coat was lovely. Doughty touched it briefly. It felt warm and thick, a soft wool, maybe cashmere. Doughty then touched his hat, while it was in the upswing. So soft. His amazing dick stayed so hard he felt it could break down walls! But it wasn't going to produce anything. When the man pulled his head up to take a breath, Doughty zipped up and went back to Beata. He was amazing. Everything was his. He loved crack. He loved his dick. He loved New York City. He wasn't just king of the castle anymore, he was the king of everything he wanted. He wanted everything. It was all his.

"I DON'T KNOW why I'm letting you come over. I sort of have a boyfriend now. Remember? We're not exclusive, but he's growing on me," she said as she unlocked her door.

Doughty did not remember because it wasn't important, and ignoring stupid things was important. He had convinced her to do some more shots as she closed up the bar, cleaning and organizing things, wiping surfaces, the endless wiping of surfaces. Creepy Joe Bird stayed with them, pulling down the gate for her, then left when Beata locked it.

"Thanks, Joe!"

"My pleasure, Bee! See you soon, sweetheart!" and off he went, finally.

The minute they were in her railroad apartment, which was all neat and dusted as poor people were wont to do, he went to her counter and, seeing a large bottle of Maker's, poured himself a big drink.

"You okay?" she said. "You seem . . . high-strung."

"I have a huge deal I tried to close before the holiday and the mortgage didn't come through. I'm just a little stressed. It's going to happen."

She gave him a look.

"I stand to make forty grand on this one."

"Wow, that's great, Doughty."

She sat down on the futon, put a pillow behind her back. "Ron is visiting his family. I miss him." That was the name of her boyfriend. He'd forgotten his name. It was best he just forget everything about him, due to his lack of importance.

"Is that your boyfriend's name? I forgot." He grunted. He was coming down hard now. Why did Beata not have any crack? Or cocaine. Oh well. He poured another big drink. "It's a terrible name."

"I don't care what you think of his name. Ron's pretty great. He's in the music business. But I'm glad we're taking it slow. Wow, you're really drinking."

He poured her a huge drink, looking at the bottle. It was half full. "Join me."

"I kind of hate the holidays," she said. She took the drink. He sat next to her. She smelled of clean young-person sweat and beer. Energy was a weird thing. He felt her energy wavering between comfort and something else. She looked straight at him. She wasn't drunk enough yet. "I think you should leave after this drink."

"We're old friends! Calm down." He drank half his drink in a swallow. He saw a bottle of NyQuil on the milk crate next to her bed, on the same Georgia O'Keeffe book that had served as the tabletop in Brooklyn. The heat was blasting through the radiators, hot and dry.

"True." She got up, stepped over him without touching him, and went to grab a tiny green-checked shift dress off the bathroom door hook. With her back turned toward him, he watched her strip out of her work clothes and pull the dress over her bird body—it was quick, efficient, like so many things she did. Then she took a large metal pail off the radiator and refilled it with water.

"Does that even help?" Doughty asked.

"I mean, I think so. It helps make steam so the air isn't as dry."

"You always wear that dress."

"It's comfortable."

He grunted again. The dress was so cheap. Everything she wore screamed "cheap." She was the opposite of Sophia. A small railroad apartment, slinging beers and shots at the only dive bar in SoHo. Probably shopped at a mall when she was home.

Again, she had her eyes on him in a way he didn't like. Her thin, wide lips pressed so hard it was just that darkish line across her big, round, profoundly young face. She looked like a cartoon. He wished he had more crack. He picked up one of her nursing books and looked at that instead of her face. He grunted as he turned the pages. He really wanted more crack.

"I'm so tired of your grunt."

"This is a psychology book! This isn't nursing. You know psychology was my major in college." He patted the spot next to him on the futon. She was standing with her arms on her hips. "Aren't you done with this shit? Now that you're a nurse."

She sat down next to him, not answering him, looking weak with exhaustion. Her dress pulled up when she sat, and he saw the white panties over her crotch. He got hard. He pulled at the strap of her dress.

"Hey," she said, but she was softening a bit. The whiskey was working on her. It was barely working on him, thanks to crack. He got up and poured a huge one.

"Jesus, Doughty," she said.

"I'm tense." He grabbed her thin wrist and put her hand on his dick.

"Stop, Doughty."

"I'm tense."

"Well then have a drink, but stop that."

"Drink with me." He took her glass and refilled it. He watched her look down at the glass, saw the part in her black hair on top of her head, the thin white scalp of it. She drank. He touched her scalp.

"Stop." She pushed his hand away.

Now he was really hard. He grabbed the drink out of her hand and put it on the Georgia O'Keeffe book and took her hand and put it on his dick. "Feel this. Feel what you do to me."

"Stop," she said, and she struggled and he grabbed her and he looked at his large hand around her tiny bird wrist and he squeezed so hard she yelped.

Then, he just lost his mind with excitement. They struggled a bit, he kept putting her hand on his dick, she kept pulling it away. It was fun, but she didn't look like she was having fun. She kept saying "Stop," so he started saying it, too! So fun! *Stop! Stop!* She tried to get off the futon but he grabbed her and he had both of her wrists now. She could fight! He watched with utmost fascination and excitement as she flailed about. Like fish out of water! Flapping around! She weighed maybe 110 pounds. He pushed her back, hard.

"Stop it."

"I can't help myself." He was over her and he let go with one hand and ripped off her underwear. He was breathing hard. Sweat dripped from his face onto hers. It was hot. It was hot from the radiator, from the struggle, and it was hot to watch her writhe. It was almost like his dick was in her already.

He leaned over and tried to kiss her but she turned her face away and he got her cheek. He went from there to her neck and licked. There was the taste of sweat. Amazing. He needed to get his pants off. This would mean letting go of her, but it was necessary. He pulled back and jumped up and took off his pants. She was quick. Up she went into the kitchen toward the bathroom door and there was no lock on it but there she went. He went after her, his magnificent dick pointing up. He swung the door open and picked her up.

It was like in the movies. Like in *An Officer and a Gentleman*. He was Richard Gere lifting Debra Winger. Like in *The Bodyguard*, he was Kevin Costner protecting Whitney Houston, the one real protector, the one to trust. The one who owned her. He carried her toward the bed and she said something but he was deep into the revelry, his mastery, the beauty of it. It was all so hot and he got her down on her back and had her wrists over her head, her whole body pinned under his larger body, and he slid into her. Despite the crack, despite the whiskey, to his great surprise, it was quick. Quick like the first time he fucked her. He came so hard, so great, her pussy was so magically tight and wet, and he came buckets inside her, falling on top of her, his dick and his whole body just jerking around as it did after a magnificent come.

He fell off to the side, breathing heavily.

She sat up. He heard a short, stifled sob. She went into the bathroom. He got up and poured another drink—the bottle was nearly empty—then flopped onto the futon. His heart was racing still. He breathed deeply. He chugged some NyQuil. When she came out of the bathroom, she sat at the kitchen table, red-faced and frowning—not her best look. Her voice cracked. "That hurt."

Doughty could barely catch his breath. Strange. He'd never felt better in his entire life, even though he wanted more crack. He'd never felt stronger or more alive until now. "Sorry." What? He never said he was sorry. Unless he added the "Not!" Whoops. So, even though he usually said it all at once, he added, "Not!" That sounded weird. So then he repeated it altogether, joyfully, "Sorry. Not!" and laughed.

He took a look at her and she looked mad, so it was time to think on his feet. His mind was on fire. He needed more whiskey, and then there was the desire for more crack. It was the best thing he'd ever had. "That was soo hot. You're amazing." He patted her leg. A compliment. That should do it. It wasn't a complete lie; she wasn't amazing, he was amazing, but it was hot. It was the perfect thing to say because of that. True, but not true. Sorry. NOT! That way, you stay in charge.

"That was awful. I want you to leave." Then she started really crying.

"Aw, come on. You loved it."

"No." She had her face in her hands now and did the shoulder-shaking-quiet-cry thing.

He was a bit annoyed. Beata was normally so stoic. Thin-lipped, hard-faced Beata. He reminded himself that he was the king of the castle. Every woman loves a fascist. "I couldn't help myself. You changed in front of me." Good God, she was being inconsolable. He got up, peed, then walked over to her and knelt next to her. He put a hand on her shaking shoulder. God, how he hated when women cried. "You're just so sexy." Then his brilliance took over. "You are one of the sexiest women I've ever met. You drive men wild and you know it." Then he said, "I love you." Now, that was every woman's dream, to hear those words. Had he ever said it? Had he said it to Sophia? He needed crack or something.

She looked up. Her face was a mess. "I need you to leave."

HE LEFT, BUT he took the NyQuil. Her face was not the face he wanted to spend the night with, so leaving was the right thing to do. No one needed to look at that. At least it wasn't far to Sophia's. She had some Xanax in her cabinet. For a moment, he thought of going to Tompkins Square Park. Was the woman still there? Amanda? In the winter? He knew there was crack there. But as he chugged the NyQuil on his way to Mercer Street, he thought, Another time. Then he had an idea, why not try Stan and Lew? Maybe they hadn't left for Darien yet? When he got to Sophia's, he called. He was in luck! He informed them he'd be there shortly. He went into the kitchen, where he hid the cash he'd hoarded under oven mitts that they had never used once, and splurged on a cab. It was almost Christmas! It was his gift to himself, because he alone was his own personal savior!

Chapter 18

When he'd spoken to Stan on the phone to inform them he was coming to visit, he could tell they'd been drinking and even though he had heard Lew loudly telling him to fuck off, he'd ignored them of course. Stan had disclosed that they'd only be going home for a long weekend, like at Thanksgiving. So when he showed up, and they answered the door, the two standing there dressed and ready to go out, he knew he'd made their night.

"Let's go out!" Doughty said. It was clear they weren't letting him in. "Let's go get last call at Dorrian's for old times' sake! Do you guys have any coke?"

"No," said Stan.

"I have a quarter ounce," said Lew.

Stan and Doughty looked at Lew. "You fucking holding out on us," said Doughty. He felt Stan on his side on this one.

"Okay, let's do it. But I'm not buying a thing all night," said Lew, and they rushed in, coats on, snorted the blow off the kitchen counter, then left.

—

DORRIAN'S HAD BEEN the classic Upper East Side underage drinking spot when they were in high school. It was an institution. Getting insanely fucked up there was a rite of passage. All of them had been there many times. For the private school teenagers of Park Avenue, it was a regular part of their gilded lives. It was as classic as going to a Yankees baseball game, not that Doughty had ever been, but he had watched a lot of Yankees games with his father. He read about baseball in the *Post*, too.

Dorrian's, where they sat that December evening, looking out on the cold night, snow hard and dirty on the street in front of them, drinking overpriced Jack and Cokes, was a piece of New York history. He scanned the room, looking for someone who could sell him coke. Maybe the bartender? It was fairly packed for the end of the night. He loved New York. He had brought two hundred dollars with him. Five years ago, when they were in high school, the famous Preppy Murder case had begun at Dorrian's. Robert Chambers, who got kicked out of Choate, a boarding school rival of Taft's and a few other schools, had gone on a date that ended with a strangulation in Central Park. He was arrested and imprisoned for it. It was still something fun to discuss, something that hung over the place. It didn't hurt the allure of Dorrian's, it made it even more rich and lovely. The owner of Dorrian's had paid Chambers's bail! Everyone knew Robert Chambers. Everyone *was* Robert Chambers. Everyone's parents had loved Robert Chambers. He was a golden child, the perfect Upper

East Side son—tall, handsome, athletic. Of course, there was the talk that he wasn't from a nice family, which was true, that he was a scholarship kid at St. David's and Choate. But he was of the world. He lived in their world. He was tall and very handsome.

After three Jack and Cokes, they did the requisite whispering about Chambers, although because they were very drunk the whispers were quite loud. They all knew people who knew him. Doughty had done coke with him once. He decided to remind his friends. He said, "I did coke with him once!"

"We know."

"I think it was because he was a Catholic," said Lew. "He had that creepy bishop gunning for him."

"His mother was super Irish, like a charwoman thing," Stan said. "I think she still lives in that town house, on Ninetieth or something."

This perked up Doughty. The living, the tragic ones left in the wake of disaster. He actually remembered where she lived! He had read all about it! And it came back to him! Her address. Everyone had known everything about him at the time. And now, he remembered. He remembered photos of the building she lived in. He loved his brain, his filing cabinet of a brain, the strange things that stayed inside it. But he was super irritated, too. He wanted some coke. "Let's go," he said. "Let's go find his place!"

They did a round of shots, that Doughty paid for even though he immediately regretted it, because he never paid as a rule, then began the walk uptown. Hunched over from the wind, hands deep in pockets.

"You know what he did that was smart?" Doughty offered. He was in the mood for some lesson-giving. It was work to share his knowledge power, to school them. But it was worth it sometimes, to expend his precious energy in this manner. "He picked a SoHo girl. A downtown girl. He picked a girl who no one cared about that much. Her family didn't have any money. Who cares? No one."

They laughed at that. Doughty didn't laugh, but he watched them laugh and a ball of comfort rolled around happily inside him. He knew things they didn't.

They were all drunk, but Doughty was the least drunk. And he really needed more cocaine if he couldn't get crack. He needed something. They walked slowly, looking up at the buildings on Ninetieth, discussing what the cross streets could be. Doughty was grinding his teeth.

"Was it between Park and Fifth?" Lew asked no one.

"What are we looking for?" Stan asked. He'd forgotten their mission.

"The building, Stan," Doughty said. "The building where Robert Chambers lived. It's a historic site."

"Is this the building? What the fuck are we doing? We should go back and keep drinking," Lew said.

Doughty stopped. "Here it is. It's this one. This is where he grew up. His mother still lives here. Doughty pointed to a window. "That's her bedroom window. Right there."

Lew looked at him. "How do you know?"

"Because I actually remember things, you retards. I remember that detail. I knew him. I did coke with him a few times at Andrew Wallington's place on Park Avenue. We bought coke from the doorman and went up to the apartment through the service elevator."

"I also thought you were lying, you lying asshole." Lew laughed.

Doughty stared at the window. "I wasn't lying." It made him happy, how little they knew. How they didn't know when he was lying or when he wasn't. They could only guess, and that was where he wanted people, forever guessing, forever not being sure.

"I still think the bitch asked for it," Stan said. "She was fucking everybody. She had that sex diary. I mean, it was an *accident*. She was the pervert. She loved getting choked, stupid slut. It just got out of hand. Got to give Chambers some credit. He got a lot of pussy."

They all nodded in agreement. This fact was basically undisputed.

Doughty crashed at their place, but he didn't really sleep. The next morning, he listened to them mill about. They both were going home, to Darien. It was 7 A.M. Stanny threw a pillow at him. "Get up, you shithead." He didn't flinch.

Lew walked over and picked up the pillow and hit Doughty over the head again and again.

"Motherfucker, get up. We have to go to work."

Doughty didn't move. He could feel Lew's rage and he felt the pillow drop on his shoulders and then Lew slapped him in the head. "GET UP! Jesus. Doughty!"

Doughty moved slowly and sat up. His ear was ringing. "Oh man, I'm hungover." He stretched.

"Are you not listening?" Lew was red-faced. "Get up."

Stanny said, "I'm leaving," and shut the door behind him.

"Hey, man, leave me your key, I'll put it under your doormat when I leave." Doughty's head throbbed where Lew had hit him.

"How am I gonna get in the building?" Lew said. "Get up! Get out of here!"

Doughty was lying down with his head turned away from Lew. "You push all the buzzers until someone lets you in."

Lew threw a key chain at him and stormed out of the apartment. Doughty heard him slam the door.

THEN, SOMEHOW, HIS body just shut down and he managed to sleep. He slept until 3 P.M. As he got ready to leave, he took a beautiful Black Watch tartan scarf that he saw hanging by the door, wrapping it around his neck. The cashmere felt so soft he made a little noise of appreciation. He walked over to an oily place on First Avenue that shined shoes, fixed umbrellas, and made keys. He made copies of all the keys and decided to invest in a new, color-coded key-ring system. He had so many keys now!

Back at Lew and Stanny's apartment, he drank a beer from their fridge and spread his purchases across the coffee table. He had a large black master ring, and on it he linked smaller, colored rings and the keys he assigned to them, blue for his mother's house and car, green for storage, red for Stanny and Lew's apartment plus Lew's house in Darien, pink for Beata, orange for Sophia. There! That was much better, and an impressive key-ring system like this made perfect sense for a young man working in real estate. He packed the other two

beers in the fridge in his backpack, then went into their bedrooms. From their bedside-table drawers, he collected a large
portion of the cash. But not all of it. Never all of it. Well, usually never all of it was a rule. It was important to leave some
for them. Mostly because he was feeling kind. But it helped in
case they decided to pretend to know how much money they
had in their bedside drawers, or how much money they had
spent last night. They had no idea. Still, better to be safe. He
left eighty bucks richer. He dropped Lew's original keys on the
kitchen table and left.

It was officially very cold. He felt his heart working hard,
his blood vessels narrowing. He started to hunch. Why did
people hunch when they were cold? To keep all the heat inside,
he reasoned with himself. But it was something he wanted to
look up in his encyclopedia or, even better, in a medical book.
He contemplated going to his storage unit and bringing his
encyclopedias to Sophia's. Maybe another day.

Chapter 19

The next day was Christmas, and he took the train to see his mother. Just one night, then back to the city. He still had Sophia's place to himself and he intended to enjoy it.

His mother, strangely, wasn't that disappointed about his brief stay. This would have bothered him, but instead, he realized he needed the freedom from being responsible for her. He had so much on his plate. And she was so boring, with Mrs. Hutton this and Mrs. Hutton that. Plus, whatever used to be mildly amusing about her when she'd been drinking like a pro was gone. To drown out her stupid chatter, he popped in a VHS tape of George Carlin's *Playin' with Your Head*.

"I know you love George Carlin, even though he's a bit vulgar for my taste . . ."

"He's not *vulgar*, Mom. He's a genius. And like me, he uses language that is necessary." He looked at the maybe two-foot-high Christmas tree she had in the corner of her apartment. It was so sad, so small, and it had a smattering of some old ornaments he remembered from his childhood. A moose hanging upside down. A reindeer. But the lights strung around the tree were just white, not colored.

"Where are the colored lights?"

"I had to downsize everything, Bobby, so I bought a short string . . ."

"Why not colored? Why just plain white?"

"I thought it was nice for a change."

"You thought wrong." He waited for her apology. She had her head tilted strangely.

"I like it. It reminds me of the tree at church. That tree just has white lights."

"It's boring. I come home for Christmas, and you can't even have colored lights for me."

George Carlin swore, and his mother did the sign of the cross. He looked at her until she looked back. "Stop, Mom. Stop ruining my Christmas."

"I'm not ruining anything and—"

"SHUT UP!"

"Mrs. Hutton says you shouldn't talk to me like that." Then she shut her mouth in a way that made him think of Beata. He felt like his head was going to explode. Ever since he'd smoked that crack, all he wanted to do was smoke crack. His mother was making him want to smoke crack.

"Mom. Mrs. Hutton or whatever you call her . . ."

"You told me not to call her—"

"ENOUGH, *Mom*. Jesus." He stood up and walked over to the kitchenette. He found a bottle of cheap whiskey under the sink and poured himself a glass. "If you're going to drink you might want to buy better alcohol. What is this?" He held the generic plastic bottle of whiskey at arm's length and then he lifted it over his head, then he waved it around a bit. "You're disgusting."

He waited. He was waiting for her to say "I'm sorry." She didn't. She just sat there with that closed-mouth thing that was bothering him. He put some ice in his glass and flopped back down onto the couch.

UPON HIS RETURN, Doughty went straight to his storage unit and tried to take a nap, surrounded by the comfort of his stuff. Christmastime was so peaceful in the storage facility. He looked at his new tape. George Carlin was an undisputed genius. He felt a great affinity for George. George and Mr. Miyagi. It was important to have heroes. He felt like he and George were soulmates, even though he didn't really believe in the soul and neither did George, which was one of the ways they were soulmates, the not believing in souls. The other was their great understanding of humanity, one that they both felt the need to share with the world. They were handsome, funny men, men who had to fight for what they believed in and never backed down.

He couldn't nap. Instead of harnessing his inner power to rest, he realized he needed to use that inner power for other things. It wasn't a failure, this not napping. Before heading back to Sophia's, he put on his puffer coat and his backpack and took an empty subway to the East Village and walked over to Tompkins Square Park to find his friend, Amanda. It had been a long time. But he hadn't forgotten her. Not forgetting someone was the best kind of flattery. It was 3 A.M., a bustling time for Tompkins Square Park. Not surprisingly, she was there, waiting for him.

"Amanda! Merry Christmas!"

"You." Her face was grim. She needed him to cheer her up. "What do you want?"

"Want to smoke crack?"

"Give me forty dollars."

He gave her a twenty.

"That's not enough for both of us."

"I'm not buying you crack."

"I'm getting you a rock, man. Get your own, then." She flung the bill back at him.

He snatched it.

"Get us both a rock. I'll watch your dog."

She sat there, petting her dog. Sometimes he felt a duty to help those who needed some guidance, but his mental self-regulation of sharing too much of his brilliance was an important thing to consider. This wasn't one of those times, a time to share his knowledge, to explain why she should do things for him. He threw another twenty at her. "You want to get high or what," he said.

She stood and walked into the maw of the park, and he sat with the dog. Tompkins Square Park was actually a beautiful place in many ways. He lit a cigarette while he waited. There was a charm to the near continuity of the not-so-secret activity, the shadows and staccato noises of people in desperation and negotiation. The hushed voices only intermittently punctuated with great chunks of noise. It was like an anthill of humans. Everyone knew that ants were amazingly brilliant insects. They knew their place, they had their jobs, they got things done. Ants—it had been a while since he'd looked up ants in the encyclopedia. Perhaps not since he was a young boy burning them under a magnifying glass on the cement of the playground. Thinking of the people around him as ants wasn't a derogatory thought. What he felt was a kind of admiration.

When she returned, they took the dog inside with them and using her beat-up glass pipe, they took turns, each smoking a rock. He explained to her all about George Carlin, and she explained to him all the rock stars she'd fucked. He explained to her she was a sad drug-addict whore, and she tried to explain she wasn't, but at that point they were starting to come down and he was angry. She said she'd been smoking crack for three days and was going to shoot up dope, did he want any? It would cost him, she said, and he wasn't interested. He had morals. No heroin.

"Give me any pills you have."

"Fuck you. Get out of my tent."

He was petting her dog. "Give me them and I'll pay you next week, after these stupid holidays. I'm closing on this huge real estate deal. I'll be back."

"Fuck you, man." She was all tied up and attempting to find a vein in her beat-up arm, which was going to be tough. He looked around her tent. It wasn't even a real tent, but it was close. There wasn't much to look through. His brain screamed for crack and he told his brain to focus on where the downers were. Amanda half slid off the large pillow thing she was propped up on, and nodded out. Perfect. There was a large black gym bag and he unzipped it. Its contents were somewhat organized and he found a pink makeup bag, and inside it were prescription bottles. She had an impressive stash. He squashed being impressed. He took three, leaving plenty behind, and went to Sophia's.

Inside his loft, he poured himself a huge Absolut Vodka, and downed two Valiums. He had bottles of Dilaudid, Valium, and Xanax. "Fuck yeah!" he said out loud. He was going to fist pump, but chose not to. After he assessed them all, he decided to keep them in his backpack. Sprawled on the couch—when was she going to replace this thing?—he put the George Carlin VHS in.

He was starting to feel normal when the tape ended and he rewound it and watched it again. George Carlin was such good company. He paced a little and decided to take a Dilaudid. Crack was something else. It wasn't like doing lines with Stanny and Lew. He rewound the battered-plants part. Then rewound it a few more times. HAHAHA. "I'd like to mention a social problem we have in this country that a lot of people don't like to talk about in public but I think it's time we face this thing head-on. I'm talking about battered plants." Doughty said the words along with Carlin. Rewind. Rewind again. "But it's true . . . there are battered plants . . . And I don't just mean physical abuse." Doughty had Carlin's voice perfect. It was more than an imitation, it was an embodiment of aligned human natures. He wanted more crack so badly. He pressed pause and took two Xanax. "But I'm talking about psychological torture. The mental abuse that we put our plants through, day in and day out." Doughty wanted to get up and rewind this part again—how many times had he watched it? He was losing count. And the light through the windows had been so bright but now it was dark and his body was ready to shut down. He walked over to the bedroom to sleep, and he fell onto the bed and slept.

Part 3

Chapter 20

After the holidays Doughty glided between Sophia's and Amanda's, with the rare visit to Stanny and Lew. Mostly, he was at Sophia's. Beata wasn't returning his calls and he was taking a break from her. He liked how busy he was, and even though Amanda was seriously beneath him, he knew she needed him, too. She really did. It was a tug on him, her need. All the needy people who needed him, needed his help. Sometimes, he had to leave people waiting, like Beata. And then there was Sophia. She was the neediest of them all. She was sick all the time and worse than ever and it wasn't fun.

She also was getting weirdly bloated and she had started occasionally making him have meals with some awful friends of hers. He had preferred their dinners alone with takeout in front of the TV. It was just more work, which he hated. They were old and painfully boring, which was work, dealing with boring humans. And they were suspicious of him and his good looks. He could see them thinking, What does he want with her? He's too handsome and young for her. Once, Sophia said, "Carol thinks you're so quiet. You are quiet when we go out with my friends."

"That's because your friends are boring," he said.

"Jesus, Doughty, then why don't we hang out with your friends? I'd like to meet at least one of them. I keep saying that."

"Yeah," he said. "You do. You repeat yourself a lot. It's boring, too. Like Carol. Is that also where you got your idea about wearing clogs? From Carol?"

He got her with that one. She got sad. She was attached to her clogs and no matter how often he told her they were not sexy, she still wore them. More than once she tried to explain they were good for her feet. He didn't even give that one a grunt.

"I know I've said this before, but it's time I see where you live, or work. It's been months now."

She was on her third or fourth drink. She was feeling it, the confidence of the booze. Although it was incredibly important not to be pushed around by her, to be the king of the castle, he got up and said, "Let me refresh that." Moments of magnanimous behavior were okay.

She handed him her glass, her eyes lighting up. "Thanks, babe."

Here was the thing: the less you did, the more attention you got for what you did. That was another thing he'd learned from his father. There was such a huge payoff for thinking and strategizing, much less for doing. But if you timed your kindness properly, it made sense in the overall strategy-making.

A problem, or rather a fact, of life, that he knew because of his acute intelligence—it was almost like an intuition of sorts, like an innate gift, like a knowledge that not even intelligence or experience could explain—was how the neediness of others was both a great boon, a great gift, and a terrible annoyance. How could it be both? This was how: it gave him the opportunity to demonstrate how indispensable he was. He was part of the fabric of Sophia's life now. He kept her company, he ate her pussy like a champ, making her sing, and he fucked her with enthusiasm. In return, he rightly lived the life he deserved. SoHo had grown on him in the past year. Did he still not aspire to a Fifth Avenue penthouse? Of course he did. He thought of his life in SoHo as a part of his youth and although he foresaw a future in a much more appropriate part of New York, uptown, the East Side, he knew that wild stories from his youthful forays into the worlds that were beneath him, like SoHo, were not a bad thing. He would always have a mysterious allure and soon this time in his life in a SoHo loft, wheeling and dealing in the real estate world, would be a part of that allure.

But the annoying things about Sophia, as much as he tried to rationalize them as part and parcel of his ambitions, were getting out of hand. He only had so much patience for her whining. He was the king of the castle, and with that title, he understood that there would be petty troubles to deal with. But her physical problems were starting to consume too much of their conversation. One Saturday, he was trying to watch the George Carlin VHS in peace after fucking all morning, and she ran to the bathroom to throw up. She threw up all the time at this point, but it was her need to talk about it afterward that drove him nuts.

"Maybe I should see a doctor."

"Baby, baby *stop*. I'm watching George Carlin. Go to the doctor, then." He looked over at her. She was shaky and pale and had some large beads of sweat on her face. She'd been in the same nightgown for what seemed like forever. Her hair was filthy. "Just have a drink. You'll feel better. Then take a shower, for God's sake."

"I can't swallow food. I'm scared."

He groaned long and hard in her direction. A groan was a long, slow version of a grunt. She was interrupting a great part of the show. Carlin was leading up to the abused houseplant riff. Doughty ended his groan to laugh along with the audience. "And apparently we also have some people here tonight from the Center for the Visually Unpleasant. Try not to look directly at those people unless you're equipped with special safety glasses." He was shitting on the people who were paying to see him! Doughty loved this. He got up and pressed pause, but he said the next line, which he had memorized, out loud to Sophia. "Try not to look at those people unless you're equipped with the special safety glasses." Saying things out loud helped him live in the skin of his heroes. Sophia was sitting in her desk chair. Ha! Like she was going to work.

"What did you say, Doughty?"

"I need safety glasses, Sophia! Look at you!" Then he did the sharp, short laugh. He was bringing out all the goods.

"I'm scared, Doughty, please." She burped and ran to the bathroom, her saggy ass jiggling behind her in her disgusting nightgown. What had happened to the silky nightie? She didn't even try anymore. Gross.

He got up and turned up the volume on Carlin. "Battered plants are part of a larger problem, as you know the overall problem is called the battering syndrome." The audience laughed. Sometimes he laughed, and other times he was one with Carlin, and he listened to them laugh, but he didn't join in, because Carlin didn't laugh. He was way more Carlin than he was the audience.

She came back with a drink and after she drank it, he glanced at her through his side-eye. He got up again, gave out a nice solid grunt from the effort, and pressed pause.

"Look. Have another drink, take a shower, and put on real clothes. Stop letting yourself go. It's unattractive. That's what your problem is."

Then she started to cry. "Will you go out and pick up some food? Anything. Pretzels? Campbell's soup?"

He looked straight at her. He watched her face change. It went from scared to desperate but also became a soothed thing, since he had looked at her and now he was about to be even kinder. "Sure." He put his hand out.

She finished her drink and went to her purse and took out forty dollars.

"I'm going to need more than that."

She went back and brought him sixty more. He turned on the show.

"Are you going out to get me the stuff?"

This time, he didn't look at her. He didn't even grunt. He just put up a hand. Carlin was talking.

From his side-eye, he saw some tears. Well, she'd learn to be more patient.

When she got out of the shower, she changed into something that resembled an actual dress, albeit one that was a loose, striped thing, not his favorite, and put on some makeup, then sat back down.

"Did you go out? Doughty, I'm worried I'll throw up in public if I go out. You said you'd go get me some food."

He almost put up his hand again, but instead, he spoke along with Carlin: "I'm going to go down to the refreshment stand and buy myself a weenie . . . Then I'm going to eat the weenie and force her to watch me."

"What did you say?"

Then he said along with Carlin, "Well your imagination runs away with you."

She got up and left. Finally. He got up, pressed pause, and went and took a long, awesome shit. Then he came back and turned on the video. After maybe ten minutes, he heard the keys in the door. He saw her out of his side-eye and her hands were empty, except for her purse, which she dropped on the ground. She ran to the bathroom and retched some more.

"I didn't make it to the store," she said when she came out.

He got up and pressed pause again. She came over and her face was funky shades of red and gray. She needed some more makeup. "Try powdering your face, babe." Then, he stretched and went to put on his shoes. "Okay. I'm going out." He had to make her wait. It was so easy yet so satisfying.

ONE THING HE knew from his time developing into a real New Yorker was that the corner stores charged far more than the larger ones that were a little farther away. There was a proper grocery store about a twenty-minute walk away. He got there and perused the aisles. Now, sometimes it was necessary to buy brand-name items. But really, as he held up the can of a lesser-known brand of chicken soup, if you looked at the ingredients, they were exactly the same. He bought off-brand pretzels and two cans of chicken soup. When he got to the checkout, he gave the cashier, who was hot actually, a hot Mexican girl, one of the cans.

"I don't need this one," he said. He was so good with money. He didn't spend stupidly. He stood outside the grocery store and smoked for a half hour. He didn't want her to think he was hurrying for her.

When he got back, she was in bed. Moaning.

"I have soup and pretzels," he said, entering the bedroom. The shades were drawn, her gown was on top of the sheets, and he saw her naked shoulders.

"Maybe you should take me to the hospital."

"You're fine."

He tossed the bag of pretzels at her, it was a good toss, and they landed right next to her. She tried to sit up and gagged. She had put a large pot next to the bed and there was some gross spit-looking stuff in it and she leaned over and spit some more. He walked around to the other side of the bed and watched her try to open the bag he'd thrown at her. It was funny. She was having trouble. He decided to help. But he watched her for a little longer. It was just too much fun, watching her. She struggled with the pretzels and picked up her vodka glass, which was now room temperature, all the ice had melted, so he took it into the kitchen, poured it in the sink, and refreshed it perfectly. This went against his rules, but so did running food errands. He was really breaking some rules today. Chin up, he told himself. His father had said this only once in a blue moon, but it came to him. Not every day is a winner, his father would say.

When he got back, she was sitting up with the bag open.

"Look! You figured it out! See. You're fine."

"I can't eat them."

"Here. I brought you a drink."

She took it greedily. She was naked. He put his hand between her legs. She was a little wet and he stuck his middle finger deep in. He got hard. He pulled the covers off, threw his pants off, and spread her legs and entered her. She moaned and put the glass down. He went in and out, leaning on her chest with each hand over a mound of tit. This was right. This felt right. In and out. She was smooth and still. He was calming her. But then she started struggling a bit. He pushed down harder on her chest.

"No! No, stop! I need to sit up."

He pulled out and sat at the end of the bed while she gagged and made a deep growling noise, reminding him of a raccoon he'd once run over in a car. She then spat into the bowl.

Doughty sighed. "You should empty that out."

"I think you should call 911."

"Baby, baby," he said. He looked down at his dick. It was soft. This was all too much. He needed some air. The loft needed some airing out and he needed to get out. He thought about opening the windows and then he decided that was a bad idea. She needed to get up and exhibit some self-care.

What was the phrase? "Ambulatory rehabilitation." That was it! The filing cabinet of his mind at use again!

"You need ambulatory rehabilitation. My mother broke her foot once and she kept wanting us to get her stuff and it was bad for her, you get it? She needed to get up and do stuff. That's how this works: to get better, you need to get up and do stuff."

Sophia turned over and moaned.

Okay, this was too much. She wasn't even listening. He needed a break.

It was time to go see Amanda. His relationship with her in many ways was the most interesting thing he had going on right now, despite that she was almost always to be found in the exact same place in the park. Her pile of goods with a tent covering it wasn't as permanent as a loft or a railroad apartment, but she had such good stuff in it. She also wasn't barfing all the time. This was what he needed. She'd be grateful for his presence. And she wouldn't be whining. He put his pants on and ran his fingers through his curls.

"I'm going to give you a moment to yourself. You need to get up. There's a can of chicken soup on the kitchen counter. I'll see you later." Then he shook her. Her arm felt clammy and hard but also like it had no muscles in it. He shook her again. Hmm. Mushy and chilly but—hard. He stopped trying to understand her arm. It was wasting time. She didn't say anything. He hated being ignored. "Remember, ambulatory rehabilitation."

Chapter 21

It was a lovely spring night. Cool and breezy, not cold, not hot. Sort of perfect. He moseyed down the East Side. He was feeling generous with himself—it had been a tough day—so he stopped at a hot dog cart and ate two hot dogs and drank a Pepsi. Everyone loved Coke and he was in the small camp of Pepsi lovers. People said that Coke was the original, or that Pepsi was too sweet, but regardless, Pepsi lovers were a smaller and therefore more interesting group of people. It was sort of like a badge of individuality. It was a very elite club, Pepsi Lovers.

As he neared Amanda's place, he surveyed the situation. There she was with her dog, Butch. He had learned her dog's name. It helped to have some nice touches like that, like learning a dog's name. Her face was its normal pale green, and her hair was in full-on dreads—something he hadn't noticed before, but he thought they were an interesting touch—and she had her hand out and was asking a man for some money. She seemed to know him? Doughty didn't understand why the hand-out gesture. When she knew someone, she shouldn't need to do that. He wanted to teach her some lessons. When he got closer, he saw the man was about to give her money and she was about to take it.

"You promise it's for dog food?" the man asked.

Inside the tent were bags of unopened dog food because the many people who knew her, who weren't themselves junkies, gave her bags of it. No one who knew her well gave her actual money. Who was he to interrupt her doing business? He stood where he was, close but not too close, and watched. She was cursing as she counted the money after the man walked away.

A funny thing happened when he knew he was going to smoke crack. It was as if he were already cracked out even though he wasn't. Just the thought of it made his heart race and his mouth go dry. He walked up to her.

"Amanda!"

She had on a coat and was shivering a bit.

"Let's party! It's been a while."

"It hasn't been that long. Do you have any money?"

He gave her forty dollars, because he was feeling generous. As he sat with Butch, waiting, he looked out on Avenue A and thought, what a lovely thing, to walk from one world to another. That was one of the countless ways in which New York was perfect. No more homogeneity of the suburbs for him!

She returned and the smoking began. She left and came back, and did that again; they haggled over money, but Doughty had so much stashed away at this point and the crack was super high-quality and he was being generous. Not only did he have some under the oven mitts, but he also kept some in a can on a top shelf that Sophia couldn't reach. Not that she even thought about it. Last he'd bothered to count it was close to two grand.

THE EVENING TURNED into the next day and they needed more crack, so they decided to walk over to one of the squats they frequented, the one on Avenue C, where she said they could get some. They'd done this before. Sexual favors were traded in one room for crack or for money, and in other rooms people lay around, passed out on junk, or sat around socializing, usually by yelling at one another, all cracked out.

Amanda went to the sex crack room and he decided to go with her. She got on her knees to blow two guys. He meandered around the house, going upstairs to another floor. What a house! So many rooms! Were there four floors? Hmm, was he on the fourth floor? It was there he met a man and decided to let the guy suck his dick for some crack money. It was a massive crack party and time warped and he decided he needed to lie down on something that wasn't bug infested. He had no idea where Amanda was and there were too many people around. When he left the building, it didn't take long to orient himself—he had a brilliant sense of direction—and he chose to walk back to Amanda's tent to see what kind of downers she had.

When he got there, it was easy enough to get in, and the dog knew him at this point so that wasn't a problem, but he noticed out of his side-eye a neighbor looking suspiciously at him. He was just standing outside his own pile of junk, smoking a cigarette. Doughty thought about saying hello. Then thought, No. He went in quickly, found the pink bag— man, she really had a great pill thing going on—and took two bottles of pills with his large capable hands. He shook them— they were not empty. As he left, the man called after him, "I'm telling Amanda!"

Doughty stopped. He looked at the man. "I fed her dog! She asked me to!"

The guy flicked the cigarette at Doughty—expertly, and Doughty gave him credit for this, he appreciated a proper cigarette flicker—hitting him square in the forehead.

"I FEED HER DOG FOR HER, YOU FUCKING THIEF," the man screamed.

Well, this he didn't have time for. He didn't have time for a fight. He had bigger fights to fight. So, like the gentleman he was, he turned on his heel, the man screaming behind him, and walked back to the loft.

When he opened the door, there was a funny smell. It wasn't nearly as bad as the crack house. But still. She needed to fire her cleaning lady. It didn't have the nostril-burn tang of strange chemicals and rat and roach shit. It smelled like bad fruit. He saw that Sophia was sleeping so he went into the kitchen, poured and downed a large vodka, and swallowed three Xanax and showered. He was still high, but the come- down was starting. He poured himself a fresh drink. Then he saw there was a full bottle of Absolut behind the one he was soon to finish off. That made him have more faith in Sophia. She wasn't totally inept. Or had he bought it for her? She was inept. That was why she needed him so much.

Then he looked in on her. She was so still in her bed. Her laziness was just too much.

"Sophia," he said. He touched her shoulder. It felt strange. Rubbery. "Sophia, wake up."

In their relationship, he sometimes tired of having to be the king, the fascist, but here he was again. It was the best natural order. The vodka and Xanax were kicking in and he needed a nap and she was in the middle of the bed. He hated it when she moved onto his side of the bed. He was ready for some rest.

"Sophia, move over," and he gave her a push, a hard push this time. No more Mr. Nice Guy. She rolled over like a piece of furniture and then he saw that her skin was grayer than usual. He shoved her over harder and it wasn't easy to get her to move. He'd give her shit about this after he slept. She needed to lose weight. After he had made space for himself, he lay down and fell into a deep, wonderful, deserved sleep.

WHEN HE WOKE, it was dark and silent. He wanted crack. He basked in the darkness for a minute, surveying his body. His heartbeat was a bit scattered. The loft smelled even worse. The clothes he'd worn back from Amanda's were not in great shape—wow, they'd really had a party!—so he needed Sophia to call the laundromat. He knew that in the kitchen there was a list on the wall with the laundromat's phone number and the cleaning lady's number. Maybe he would do Sophia a favor and call the laundromat to come and pick up a bag of laundry. He breathed in and out from his mouth. "Sophia?" He nudged her. Nothing. He grunted even though she wasn't awake. He realized the grunt was also something he did for himself, and that was fine.

After peeing, he went into the kitchen and poured himself a vodka. He'd had such a great time he'd lost track of the days, which was the sign of a truly wonderful time. He saw the answering machine blinking with the number seventeen. Good God.

"Sophia!" he yelled. Nothing from her. He was not her secretary. This was not his job, looking at her answering machine.

He went back into her bedroom and stood over her. "SOPHIA! Wake up! This is too much!" He pushed her, but nothing. Nothing! Had she stolen his rock ability? Impossible! He went into the living room and drank. Cunt, he thought. He turned on the television and watched the news. Bad things were happening. For some reason, without her annoying him while he watched the news, he enjoyed it less. This, though, made him laugh. Then he got angry.

He went back into the kitchen, raging, poured another vodka, and sat down next to the stupid answering machine and decided to listen to the messages. He pressed play. He was going to give her hell when she woke. He'd make her cry. He hadn't done that in a while.

"Hey, Sophia, just checking in, it's Miranda. Where are you?"

"Sophia, this is Carol. You didn't call in sick or anything. Please let me know what's going on."

"Sophia? I'm getting worried. I came by and rang your buzzer. Where are you? Are you okay? Call me."

"Sophia, it's your mother . . . blablabla. A few of your

friends and someone from your work called me. I don't even know how they got my phone number."

"Sophia, if you don't call me back, I'm calling 911 tomorrow morning. I'm scared sick. I hope it's not that guy you're seeing. Call me!"

Well, it was worse than he'd thought. She'd officially become the laziest person he'd ever met. She hadn't even checked her phone messages? This was too much. He went out onto the fire escape and smoked cigarettes to collect his thoughts. He was very angry at her and his anger was understandable. He also knew that anger needed to be tempered to be used properly. He really wanted some crack and then he remembered that one of the bottles he'd taken was Ritalin, which was obviously bullshit compared to crack, but it was something. He smoked and took most of the pills—he counted out five twenty-milligram tablets, leaving two rattling in the bottle— washing them down with the rest of the vodka.

He was ready to confront her.

As he poked at her, her skin was doing even weirder things. It was perfectly cool, which was nice—not too cold, not too hot, sometimes her skin was really hot, which was not fun—and when he pushed it down, it really stayed down. He watched and watched and it took what seemed like forever for it to come back to its natural place. He did that a bunch all over her. Her cheeks. Her arm. He leaned into her neck and inhaled. A sweet smell—a sickly sweet smell—was coming from her. Was she wearing a new perfume? It wasn't so bad, actually. When he was in the kitchen, he had noticed she hadn't taken out the garbage, but he'd had an inkling that the garbage was not the primary source of the smell. Of course he was right, his inklings were always right, and in that way they weren't really inklings, they were just knowledge.

"Sophia!" He now moved her very aggressively, and her eyes sort of opened. He leaned over her mouth and put his nose basically in it. Nothing. Strange.

He went back into the kitchen and climbed out to the fire escape and smoked. The Ritalin was helping a little, but boy oh boy was it not crack. He took the last two. On the list next to the phone, there were some numbers of her friends. He didn't really remember many of them, but that woman named Carol had called a lot. He didn't want to be impulsive, but he decided to reach out. A tiny little bit of hesitation sparked in his head and then he remembered—I am the king of my castle. Then he dialed.

"Hi, Carol, this is Robert Savile, Sophia's boyfriend. I just got home from a business trip and it seems as if Sophia is very sick or something. I noticed you called?"

"Oh my God. What is wrong with her?"

"I'm not sure. Perhaps you should come over. I can't seem to wake her. She probably was just drinking. She seems very passed out."

"I'm getting a cab now."

He'd been so busy and had slept so well the night before, or the day before, or whatever it was, that he hadn't put on his watch so he went and got it from the table next to his side of the bed. He had slept so well. He loved his body's ability to rejuvenate like that. He was feeling better than usual now. It was 11:17 A.M. It was a Wednesday. It was March 4. With all he was doing these days, it was easy to lose track of what day of the week it was, or even what week it was. He took a quicker shower than usual in case Carol was going to be over fast—he didn't know where she lived—and got dressed in some things that were clean. It was almost his last clean outfit and he felt a surge of anger at Sophia for not having called the laundromat for a pickup. While he was at the sink brushing his teeth, the buzzer rang. They were almost out of toothpaste, he really had to squeeze to get the least little bit out of it. She'd become useless. He was done with this behavior, this absentmindedness. He brushed as best he could, and then he chewed a Xanax. He liked that when you chewed them, the nice calm came quickly, as opposed to swallowing them, which took forever. Doughty didn't have forever. He had things to do.

"Who is it?" he asked into the intercom.

"It's Carol!!"

He buzzed her up.

NOW HE REALLY remembered her from the lunches. She was a large, short, and unattractive woman, with thick black hair and a small chin, who also worked in publishing and often brought up Yale this and Yale that. And yes, Carol was the one he particularly blamed—it was really Sophia's fault, he knew; she was a grown-up, even if she wasn't acting like one now, and she made her own decisions—for Sophia's terrible choice of loose dresses and her dumb clogs because there she was, this Carol, wearing the same uniform of middle-age decay. He remembered one particularly boring dinner where they got drunk and talked about some author, DFW this and DFW that, whoever that was, and he just went out and smoked a lot. Doughty knew Carol didn't like him, but none of Sophia's friends did, and he didn't like them back, and that was the order of things. Sophia, yes. Her friends, a solid no. That was too much. Too much to ask of him. None of her friends were getting their pussies eaten out nonstop by a hot young man with a great dick and that was the resentment. They were so jealous. If he were to reach inside their sagging, gross crotches, he'd pull out fistfuls of cobwebs. It was part of his burden, being hot, making other women envious. Nothing he couldn't handle.

Carol came running from the bedroom to the kitchen and slipped on something and went down hard on her ass. Then she stood and stumbled to the window of the fire escape, where Doughty was sitting calmly, smoking and watching her, and she tilted her head back like she was encased in a roaring bear costume or something and she wailed, "She's dead! Oh my God, she's dead." Then, even though he was still right there on the fire escape, she looked at him and screamed, "I'm calling 911!" Then she ran out of the apartment, slamming the door obnoxiously, and he heard her running down the stairs, screaming, "Help! HELP!!"

THIS WAS WHERE his rock-solidness became a golden virtue. He went into the living room and sat on his couch. He became heavy, channeling his heaviness. He thought— it had a been a while, he'd been on a Carlin kick, so it was okay that it had been a while—of *The Karate Kid*. Of Mr. Miyagi. "Secret to punch, make the power of whole body fit into one inch, here." He thought about the whole power of the body. What he did was take Mr. Miyagi's understanding of power and make it an even greater strength. He took the whole power of his body and became unmovable. He was the owner of body power. He controlled his body power to a deep stillness.

But before he did that, he went into the kitchen and erased all the messages on the machine.

The EMTs came and wanted to take the body but there was a discussion of a possible crime scene. Then the police were there. One policewoman was trying to calm Carol—good luck with that—while questioning her. She was pointing at him and saying, "Doughty blablabla" and "That guy mwamwa."

He had also retrieved his backpack before returning to the couch and resuming his composure of a solid rock. Two policemen asked if he'd come down to the station.

"My girlfriend just died."

"Actually, she didn't *just* die. She's been dead for possibly three days. We'll know a lot more soon. We just have some questions."

"I'm in no shape to move, sir." People who wore uniforms appreciated being called "sir" or "madam." He did it to placate them. "I need to sit here. This is my home."

"Okay, sir, we understand." It was as if the policemen were stealing his moves. One just sat there. The other stood like a tree. A tree with no wind, he thought, channeling the words that he thought Mr. Miyagi would use.

"Do you want to call someone?"

What a silly question.

"Have you called someone?" the standing policeman asked. "We can always check the phone records later, so better to just tell us the truth."

"I have not called anyone," Doughty said. Then he was silent. They *wanted* him to call someone. Ah. Okay. This, he would do. "May I?" he asked, again with deference. These guys loved him.

"Sure." The standing policeman turned and watched him walk across the loft. He could feel the eyes on him, but he was okay with that. He had done nothing wrong. He was being so respectful. Dutiful, even.

He went to the kitchen and called the Prince Street pay phone number, let it ring six times, then hung up. He thought about calling Beata. Her number he remembered as well. Instead, he dialed his pay phone number a few more times and then he went and sat on his couch again.

He wanted to ask a bunch of questions, but ancient solid rocks don't speak. He kept repeating this to himself. Ancient solid rock no talk. No words come from rocks.

HE PAID ATTENTION to all the details of all the things: the comings and goings. Carol was taken away. Eventually, Sophia was taken away, covered in a dark zipped-up bag on a stretcher. There was yellow tape across the bedroom door and the bathroom door—thank God he knew how to hold it in, he did need to pee—and in the kitchen. The kitchen's being taped off was sort of problematic.

"Can you guys get me a drink?" At least he had his back-pack.

"Mr. Savile, we can't do that." He had agreeably shown them his expired driver's license from Connecticut. "But we can go to the station now and get you some snacks. A soda. It's been a while now. Let's go. Let's make this easy."

"I'm a Pepsi fan. I'm also from Darien." It was that time, the time to remind people from where he came. He always tried not to have to remind people of this, but sometimes it was necessary.

"I love Pepsi, too," said the cop who had a sympathetic, sad smile. The other looked stern. The smiling cop had asked to see his backpack. Doughty had done a mental accounting of all the things that were in there and he did not want them looking at the prescription bottles, so he politely declined. Doughty knew he had doctor-patient privilege, but he decided not to invoke that. He gauged how old the cop was. Who knew. Also, maybe the cop was saying that just to—pretend to be his friend?

Cops made him think of cop movies. That was pretty much all he thought, that movies made it seem like their lives were exciting and that they were heroes. But here they were, in his loft, because of hysterical Carol. Overseeing a bunch of nothing.

THE STATION WAS as bad as it was in the movies. No—it was worse. Everything was smaller, everyone who was there seemed bored. Doughty tried to channel the movie vibe of his current situation to get some entertainment from it. As he sat there, waiting for God knows what, he decided to relive the moments when they'd all left the loft together. He wanted to close his eyes to do that, but he did no such thing. Not a good idea to close his eyes. So, with his eyes open, he went into his brain and shut out everything else.

There had been a small crowd outside. A spark of reality had hit him when he stepped out—he was famous. There were photographers! He didn't smile. Funny how it is, though, he thought: when someone takes your photo, there's this impulse to turn and smile, but Doughty wasn't impulsive. He looked down, then he decided to look straight ahead, but away from the cameras. That was what famous people did. He was a famous person, and he, too, was tired of the spotlight.

At long last he had access to a toilet in the station. While on the toilet, he grabbed a Dilaudid from his backpack and took a huge shit, a really good shit. Then he was directed into a small room where he now sat on a hard-backed chair in front of an unoccupied desk with two empty chairs on the other side. Every time he looked at his Hamilton, only a few minutes had passed, so he decided to stop looking. He was suffering. But he was a rock. He stood up at one point, put on his backpack, and came out of the room to use the bathroom again because by that time they'd given him three Pepsis and a bag of Ruffles potato chips.

In the bathroom, with his backpack still on, he took another dump, a decent-size shit, not quite as large and satisfying as his first. The toilet stall was quite clean and he was happily surprised at how well his digestion worked despite the stressful situation. Then, on his walk back to the room, past the rows of ugly desks with men in bad suits on the phone or scribbling something down, one or two looking at him briefly, he noticed it was dark out now. He felt tired. It was hard being such a solid person. Finally, the same two policemen came in and sat across from him.

They asked how long he had lived at 12 Mercer Street and he said fourteen months. He was asked where he'd met Sophia and he said Lucy's. And so on. He told them he was in real estate, that he had his own real estate company. They asked him the name of it, and he said Savile Realty, and that it was very new, a new venture. And so on. At the end, the Pepsi-loving cop sat down with him, alone.

"The preliminary autopsy shows that Sophia died of acute pancreatitis from long-term alcoholism. She went into organ failure."

Doughty must have looked a bit shocked or something, because he heard "Mwamwa so sorry blabla you can go, we're in touch with her family and mwamwa blabla. We will contact you if we have any other questions."

"You've got my number," Doughty said. He'd given them the number for his loft. They even apologized for keeping him so long. As they should have.

AS HE WALKED back to his loft, he berated himself for not being entirely sure what the pancreas was. He would look that up in the dictionary. Or better yet, the encyclopedia when he went back to his storage unit. Although he was fairly certain he didn't have "P" with him. That one was still at his mother's place. He really wanted to visit Amanda. He thought: Crack. Crack crack crack. He looked at his watch. He'd been at the station for eleven hours! He deserved a crack night. But he was the newly minted sole owner of a loft in SoHo. He wanted to check on his property. He wanted to check on Sophia's, now his, investments! A million dollars! A loft in SoHo! Finally, his time had come. He went into a liquor store and was going to buy a jug of cheap vodka but remembered Sophia wasn't home, so he bought some Maker's. It had been a grueling day.

When he got there, it still smelled bad. He found some lavender Glade in the bathroom. Most of the yellow tape was gone and he sprayed the loft and took down the rest of the tape. He went straight to her filing cabinet and took out the folder with her trust statements. He carefully took the most recent one, noting it was from January, folded the thick thing in half, and put it in his backpack. He had so much on his mind and he wanted crack so badly that he would deal with that windfall later. He was a rich man with a loft in SoHo.

But then he decided to unpack some of his clothes and other things from his backpack. Why not? He lived alone now. He even folded the pair of pants and the two T-shirts— a stupid thing, folding, but since no one else was around to do it for him, here he was doing women's work—and put them in the dresser with her underwear. Then he stopped and thought, She doesn't need these, and he tossed the underwear in the kitchen garbage. He looked around the loft for a moment, then counted out five hundred dollars from the oven mitts.

He called Beata and got her answering machine. It had been so long and now that his life had taken this amazing turn, he could really use her cleaning skills. It was 3 A.M.

"Beata, I bought a loft near you. Call me! 255-3767. Write

that down, Beata. It's been too long. I know it's late, so maybe I'll stop by tomorrow and check in on you."

He started realizing there were many things that he no longer needed. He began throwing out all sorts of stuff—makeup, her toothbrush. He kept the shampoo and soaps and cleaners. The towels, too. Her closet was overwhelming. He would need to fill many garbage bags. Should he go smoke crack before the task, or after? Crack as a reward, or crack to help him focus on the work ahead? This was a tedious job, a job made for someone less important. Beata would be great. She was born to bend over and clean things. She came from a long line of women who had strong backs from scrubbing floors and whatnot. But she hadn't been easy to get in touch with for a long time now. She did have her moments of ingratitude. At this point, it had been months.

He went out onto the balcony and smoked a cigarette. It helped him focus and he decided to get Amanda. He had mixed feelings about bringing her over. She might be a good cleaner, but she might not be.

Beata was made for cleaning up after others. The ancient charwoman lineage inside her stalklike body. What was bartending? Tending to others, cleaning up their glasses, wiping down surfaces. She surely knew folding, too. She would be of great use. Plus, all the trust they'd built up over their long friendship would probably make for an even greater kind of cleaning. But first, Amanda. Why not give her a shot?

Chapter 22

"Hey, Doughty. Did you steal my pills?"

"Amanda. Let's go to that squat you took me to. You look like shit." He had perhaps jumped the gun by telling her the truth about her looking like shit, but whatever. The extra business of the past few days had rattled him a bit. He was tired and overexcited and he needed a break from all the hard work. He worked so hard. After he smoked some crack he'd go to his storage unit and move all his stuff into his loft. He had so much to think about. Then he remembered he hadn't paid for the storage since the first month so it was most likely padlocked, so he'd need something like four hundred dollars to get in. He then calculated that even though it was padlocked, he had six weeks before they threw out his stuff. He was rich and it wouldn't be a problem, but first, he needed a break from thinking. Resting the mind was as important as using the mind. Was that Miyagi? "Resting the mind is as important as using the mind," he said to Amanda.

"What? Doughty, I don't have time for your nonsense. I

need a downer. Do you have any? Someone stole mine. Or we could buy some heroin."

"Let's go to that squat. We can figure it out there."

They decided to go to the building on Third Street, which he learned was nicknamed "Bullet House," and after smoking a rock, he decided to pick the brain of a man named Blake, since he was the owner of the squat. In his late twenties, originally from Los Angeles, Blake, despite some questionable tattoos and his childish attachment to his skateboard, would be able to dispense some knowledge to Doughty. During this visit, he learned that Blake, referring to himself as the manager of the building, was the lead singer in a band called Headbreak. Doughty explained he had inherited a loft, but he didn't want to tell Blake too much because he didn't know him very well. He learned that Blake did not smoke crack, or shoot up heroin, but he used to, and now he was a thing called straight edge, which was a better way to stick it to the Man. They had a long conversation about sticking it to the Man. Doughty wanted to quote George Carlin and started to talk about George Carlin.

"George Carlin said, 'Fighting for peace is like screwing for virginity,'" Doughty said. He was starting to come down. He needed to find Amanda to come clean. He needed more drugs.

"I'm all about the fight. I'm all about fighting the Man," said Blake.

He realized that Blake was hopeless on larger issues of the human race if he didn't agree with George Carlin. Doughty was hoping to get more information about practical things. Blake kept talking about the revolution and music. He even got his guitar out. This wasn't working. He went to get Amanda. She was passed out, but he shook her awake and off they went.

The night had ended the next day around 3 P.M. and Doughty was anxious to check on his loft. But Doughty had made some decisions thanks to Blake. The information he squirreled away as he walked back to his home, coming down terribly hard from the crack: he needed a lawyer. And he had a card of a highly recommended lawyer from Blake in his pocket. He and Blake were going to have the same legal representation.

He'd had a productive day. He had accomplished a lot. They stopped by Amanda's tent and he, always the gentleman, watched her feed Butch. When she went to take Butch to the nearby dog park, he went into her hovel and opened her pink pill-stash purse. Fuck, she really didn't have any left. He went to a liquor store and bought a small plastic bottle of vodka. Sophia had been such a bad influence on him, but here he was, wanting vodka. When Amanda came back, the time had come so he said, "Amanda, I have a great opportunity for you. Come see my new loft. I need you to clean it for me."

"Do you have any drugs?"

"I do."

After she fussed over her dog, they walked to Mercer Street.

"You live here?"

"Yes. I own this loft."

"Wow." Amanda walked to the kitchen, peeked out the window that led to the fire escape, turned around, and walked to the front of the loft that faced Mercer Street, then headed back and went straight into the bathroom. She was looking for drugs. What few he had were in his backpack and he was saving them for himself so he could go into his deep sleep.

"I need some downers," she said.

She was searching the bathroom cabinet. Good luck, Amanda, he thought. In the kitchen, he poured vodkas for both of them. Then he poured them some Maker's. She gulped hers down and then rudely helped herself to some more. It was okay. He understood. He was ready for a rest. He examined his loft through her eyes from where he sat on his couch. She was impressed. He was impressive. She did have terrible manners. She yelled from the kitchen, "You have fifteen messages on your answering machine."

Strange. He had erased them all just the other day.

He was about to raise his voice and give her instructions from where he sat, but instead he started toward the kitchen and spoke calmly. He needed calm. He needed drugs but didn't want to get caught by Amanda looking through his backpack. In a flash of brilliance, he remembered there might be one bottle of pills in the side drawer of his bedroom. Of course he was right. His brain file didn't fail him. Of course it didn't fail him. He chewed two morphine pills—there were three left—and went for the vodka. She was sitting there, drinking and scratching her skin.

"Amanda, listen to them for me."

"What?"

He refilled her drink. She was scratching a purple thing on her face.

"There," he said, pointing to the notebook and pen on

the small table next to the phone. "Listen to them and then write down the calls." She looked confused. "Be a good girl, Amanda. Think of your dog."

"What? What does Butch have to do with this?"

"Because he's your dog and you care about him." He was angry and tired. He couldn't keep educating her. He needed to rest his brain. "Just do that for now. I'll let you know what else to do later." The morphine hit him. "I need to sleep. You can join me when you are done." When he woke, he'd be less kind and more like a dictator. He'd be what she needed him to be and what he needed to be, and all would be well, he thought as he heard the answering machine from the kitchen go blabla. Then, he passed out.

When he woke, Amanda was passed out next to him. She had found the pills.

Chapter 23

Harold Resnik was his lawyer. He knew he was in good hands because he was a Jew, and it was necessary to have a Jew lawyer. Resnik had an office on the edge of China-town, near city hall on the Bowery. It was in a storefront that he shared with a bail bondsman. He made an appointment, showed up five minutes early so he could smoke a cigarette, then as he reached for the door, he saw Harold approaching to open it for him. Nice. He shook hands with his attorney, keeping his side-eye on the foyer as he followed him into the office, where Harold closed the door behind them. After a brief discussion of the issues at hand, Harold asked, "Do you get mail at the apartment?"

Doughty heard the question. But he was thinking, there was a safe in the bottom drawer of Resnik's desk. He focused on a framed photo on the desk of Harold with a wife-looking person and two small children.

"Yes," said Doughty. "Lots of mail."

"How long have you lived there?"

"Years. Over two years." Then he nodded at the photo. "Lovely family."

Resnik gave him a look. "Then you are officially a tenant. New York state law states that if you have lived there for over thirty days, you are a legal tenant."

"Well that's great news." Doughty recrossed his legs. It was important for circulation, to recross one's legs, to not keep them crossed the same way for long. Ideally, he would sit wide-legged, but he was being extra polite. "Any way to get a coffee here?"

"No," said Resnik. Funny, thought Doughty. He had seen a coffee machine in the foyer. "Any bills in your name?"

Doughty took a moment. "I would need to check. I want the deed to the apartment in my name. Blake said something about that to me and I think that's a great idea. What about a Pepsi?"

"To be the legal owner of the property, you can make an adverse possession claim after ten years of occupancy."

"That's excellent news."

Harold gave him the same look he'd been giving him for a while. He didn't appreciate being looked at like that. Why did people do that and think they could get away with it? It didn't help their cause and it didn't make him like the man. He had to do some schooling. "Harold. I am an expert in real estate. I sell houses in the West Village and now I have this loft. Getting this loft in my name, making me the owner of the property—that's your expertise."

Harold looked down at his large desk calendar. Doughty saw that he had many appointments written down. Doughty was looking at them, trying to read the names, as Harold kept talking. "Utilities. Robert? If you have a utility bill in your name that's always helpful."

"I can do that."

There was some more discussion and Doughty was getting the itch from sitting so long. He wanted a little hit of crack. Just a little. Not a whole rock.

Resnik handed him some paperwork to sign.

He looked at Harold and raised his hands up. "Harold, Harold." Repeating someone's name always gave one an edge. "Harold. What is this?"

"Like I said, I need a down payment if you want me to do further work on this. Another thing to consider is to negotiate a buyout. If you don't have any money, I can negotiate with your landlord to pay money—usually a substantial sum—to get rid of you. Then you need a different contract, one that gives me twenty percent of that buyout, but you don't have to give me anything up front."

"Blake explained to me that you do pro bono work."

"I do, for tenant-eviction cases. But you said you own a loft on Mercer Street. So."

"Let me rephrase." Doughty sat silently. He was deep in his mind. He had the investment-account papers in his backpack, proof of his inheritance, but he knew that this Jew lawyer would then try to get him to pay. And he wanted this work pro bono. If Blake had gotten him to work for free, why would he pay this man? He would call the bank later. One thing he knew about money was that you never told anyone you had it. Only poor people told you how much money they had, which was why they were poor. He was from generational wealth, so money belonged to him, and it was nothing you ever talked about. Thank God for his Darien upbringing. While he was thinking warmly of his entitled wealth, Harold had more things to say, and was saying them. Doughty summoned up all his patience while not listening. As he left, without signing anything but with paperwork in hand, he thanked Harold. "I'll be in touch."

"Here," Harold said, and handed him more stuff. It was as if he wanted Doughty to do his work for him. This was the problem with a large part of humanity. No one wanted to do the work.

"Here's some information on squatter rights and other rights regarding renting properties in New York City. Maybe you'll find this helpful. If you do want me to work for you, you're going to need to give me more information and bring in some mail with your name and your address on it. That would be the start."

Harold reached down into a filing cabinet, on the other side from where the safe was, and pulled out a stapled document. "Take these, too. And if you want to try to get the owner of the building to give you a bunch of money to leave, let me know. We can do that. Very common."

"I'm not going anywhere, but thanks."

ON HIS WAY out, he took note of a framed photo of an ocean, its waves reaching toward the sand. The wood paneling. The windows needed a wash. He understood. It wasn't easy getting good help. The once-empty desk facing the street he'd walked by on his way through the foyer was now occupied by a woman in her early forties with a chest so square it went from her neck to her waist. She did not have on a wedding band. He stopped to introduce himself to Teresa, which was her name, according to her nameplate on the desk. He decided to acknowledge the lowly secretary, because sometimes it was good to be familiar, friendly, with the help. It made them more secure in their position. It kept them happy, little acts of "I'm just like you!" Even though, clearly, they were not like each other. Her suit was 100 percent polyester.

"Nice suit!" he said. "Do you have any Pepsi? I'm a new client of Harold's."

"No," she said. "Have a good day."

When Doughty left, he walked up the Bowery, past all the chandelier stores, and he took an inventory of himself. Though intellectually he knew that the winds were turning in his direction, he wasn't feeling it. He didn't feel much of anything. He wasn't sure what to feel, so he decided to figure it out. Feelings needed intellect to make them the right feelings. Something as hard as the hardness that already was part of his innermost self got heavier. He almost had to stop walking, which he did when he got to a busy intersection. The light was red. The cars passed in front of him. People were waiting impatiently, standing over the curb of the sidewalk and right on the street. This was a dumb thing to do. The two steps into the street gave them pretty much zero advantage. It showed weakness. Because it showed impatience.

Doughty remained flat-footed on the sidewalk, at least two

feet away from the street. Cars honked. He closed himself up in his hardness.

Here was the thing. He was owed. Everything—everything that came his way—was his. His inheritance. This was one of the moments, like all the moments in his life, one after another, of what he deserved. Something like joy began to feel like liquid in him, so when the light changed and it was time to cross, he solidified himself. He crossed the street with the power of an outer space extraterrestrial rock so heavy it crushed the earth beneath his feet.

Chapter 24

It became summer quickly, as it does in New York City. First it's cold, then it's hot. Spring is a fleeting day or, if lucky, week. The phone in the loft no longer worked. He contemplated calling the phone company, but there was his trusty pay phone on the corner of Prince and Mott, right near Beata's. Beata. She *still* hadn't returned his calls. And every time he knocked on her window, she didn't come to the door. Once, he could see her in there, and she still hadn't come out. He didn't know what to think. He wasn't going to make a scene, bang on the window like a person on drugs. Or scream or anything. What was her problem? Clearly, she'd lost her mind. He'd gone to Milady's once and seeing she was behind the bar, decided to go in to say hello, but Joe Bird was outside smoking and he said, "Hey there. You can't go in there."

Doughty had calmly pulled out a cigarette and stood his ground. Joe was looking at Doughty with his bloodshot eyes, the redness making the blue glow as it often did, all wet and shiny. His eyes were impressive.

"Oh yeah. Why not?" He smiled at Joe. Joe Bird. Thick and fattish, his hair like a Brillo pad. How old was he? Maybe he was old. God knows. His face was as red as a beet.

"Because I said you can't!" Then he laughed, revealing his gross mouth, the fangs around the empty place where his teeth should be, his tongue a reptile-monster thing. Clearly, he hadn't learned the importance of not showing his teeth, of covering them with his lips while laughing. Doughty laughed along with him—the right way. A deep, manly laugh. He was trying to show how a man laughs to Joe via example. Joe didn't pick up on his hint. He was trying to help the man, but Joe just stood there, smiling. Well, the working class were a different breed. Manual labor made people gross. Doughty sighed, put out his smoke, and opened the door to go in.

"Hey there, buddy." Joe grabbed his arm, and not gently. This, Doughty did not like. He wasn't going to shake him off, this wasn't necessary. He just stood still. Always the rock. "You want to go for a ride in my van? Or you wanna get the fuck away from here?"

This was deeply sad. He really didn't have anything else to do, poor ugly Joe, but pretend to be a bouncer. He wasn't a bouncer, this Doughty knew for certain. Beata had told him that Joe didn't officially work for Milady's, he was just a friend of the family's, a friend of the bar's, as if that were a thing. He supposedly captured and killed pigeons, which he put in the back of his van and sold to restaurants in Chinatown. Doughty had never seen him do it. Beata claimed to have seen it. She claimed that once when she'd expressed disbelief to Joe, on a quiet day during a day shift, Joe took her outside and whistled a special whistle. Then a pigeon fluttered to the ground. Beata said he was so quick she didn't see him lean over and grab it, but he must have, because the next thing she knew, he was holding the bird next to his chest, the neck cleanly broken, no blood, no squeal of pain, just dead in his hand.

Doughty stood so still and so solid that the time would come when Joe's grip would loosen. He could wait. He saw the back of Beata's head from where he stood. He thought of Mr. Miyagi. He thought—and this got him a bit excited and his arm moved a little, which made Joe grip it tighter—maybe Joe dealt drugs, too. "You don't happen to have any crack on you, buddy, do you? Or anything?"

"If I did, I'd shove it down your throat. Would you like that? A fist down your throat? I bet you'd like that, Dotty. I can make that happen." He started laughing more and for whatever reason this made him grip Doughty's arm so hard that a tick of impatience came over Doughty. "All right, buddy? You got that? BUDDY. I can shove my fist down your throat now for practice, you want that, buddy?"

The unpleasantness was too much. "Joe, I have somewhere to be. I need to go."

"I bet you do. You just go. You do that. You go where you're needed." And he let go.

DOUGHTY DIDN'T LET that incident bother him for more than a minute. He did decide that it was time to really pursue Beata more, as Amanda was slightly unreliable, even though they had been hanging out together a lot. Beata was the epitome of reliable. She was born to show up on time and start cleaning or cooking or serving. Her ancestors had had no choice and this was a genetic thing inside her. She was like a good horse. She was a good horse. A good bird horse. He dropped the line of thought, lit a cigarette, and moved forward, walking in the lovely night air. At night, it wasn't as hot. He'd become a night owl, walking the streets of his city, the city that never sleeps, safe from the suffocating heat, the sidewalks empty of all the people going to and fro for their nine-to-five jobs, their errand-running, and lunch and dinner dates. Yes, nighttime was the time for people like him. People who couldn't be bothered with the ordinary and mundane.

As the days went on, he realized he also had let his friendship with Stanny and Lew falter. He was so busy for one, and they also hadn't been picking up when he did call from the pay phone. Finally, he got Stanny to pick up. It was midnight on a Tuesday. Stanny was drunk, but they made plans for him to come downtown the next night for dinner. Stanny informed him that Lew had moved back to Darien and was commuting. This didn't surprise Doughty. Many young men from the suburbs ended up back home, back in their comfort zone. Not everyone was cut out to make it in New York. Stanny had a new roommate, an old classmate from the University of Vermont. And so on and so on and blablabla. Doughty smoked and listened for as long as he could stand it. Then he turned the conversation back to him. He explained he now was studying law. And helping out people who were having difficulty with their mortgages. It was part of the many things his company did.

"Really, dude? You've never been the charity kind of guy.

What the hell? Did you find God or something?" Stanny laughed.

"Stan, at some point, when you're successful enough, you have to have a charity arm. It's a great way to meet people, for one."

That seemed to sober up Stanny a bit. "Do you go to the Met Gala and shit?"

"Of course I do. When I have the time."

"Wow."

"So come by tomorrow and see my loft in SoHo, then we'll go out, downtown. I'll show you around."

"I thought you owned a house in the West Village."

"I sold that. You really need to invest in my company. You wouldn't need roommates if you were making real money. I'd let you invest, if you want."

"I like having a roommate, we have fun together. Mwamwa . . ."

Doughty wanted crack. Stanny was stupid and boring. Doughty was loyal, but this was enough. "I gotta go, dude. See you tomorrow!"

HE SLEPT HIS sleep that night with the help of some vodka and some pills. When he woke, it was because his buzzer was ringing like mad. This wasn't good. He looked at his watch. It was nine in the morning? What was this? He needed more sleep. He had gotten in bed at 5 A.M. He lay back down and closed his eyes and his ears.

People who leaned on buzzers were a strange breed. Like children, they thought that being incredibly loud and obnoxious would get them results. He was in the mood to go smoke crack with Amanda, who had been somewhat helpful the last few times she'd been over. It took some training, and she wasn't great, but she was learning. He'd gotten more pills from her. He'd had to pay for them, but he had some regulars at the piers now and any day he'd get that trust put in his name. She cleaned his bathroom, not as well as Beata would have. But someone had to wipe off the dried piss from the toilet seat. He quoted George Carlin out loud to himself to counteract the stupid buzzer noise. "Think of how stupid the average person is, and realize half of them are stupider than that." The buzzer was no longer an on-and-off-again thing, it was just a single noise.

Well, he'd get more of his deep rock sleep later. He got up and turned on the Carlin video and sat on the couch. One thing still irked him—a few things, but one thing for sure: the couch. Why Sophia had never gotten a sectional was beyond him. He turned up the volume to fight the buzzer noise.

Then he refocused on Carlin. The man was such a genius. He was a hero of the intelligent people, people like himself. The masses? They were to be dealt with for who they were. Stupid. He was with Carlin. He was one of the not-stupid people.

He decided to leaf through the pamphlet on squatter rights while whoever leaned away on the buzzer leaned away. Now that it wasn't an on-and-off-again noise, just a long, endless buzzing, he had adjusted to it. He hadn't looked at the pamphlet in a while. Of course, he had understood it all the first time he'd leafed through it, but it was a good distraction while the buzzer buzzed. He thought of it as prep work for when law school started. As he flipped the pages around, he thought of another Carlin quote that he'd held close to his heart and repeated to himself with regularity: "Life gets really simple once you cut out all the bullshit they teach you in school." This warmed him. It was important for him to have a few like-minded people in his midst, and Carlin was one of them.

The buzzing had stopped and he decided to go have a cigarette on the fire escape. As he walked to the other end of the loft and climbed out the window, an excessive knocking on the door began. He stood very still on the fire escape and smoked. In New York, it happened. People knocked on the wrong doors all the time. Once, he'd almost gone to the wrong tent to find Amanda. But, like Carlin, he was not most people, so he'd found the right tent quickly. Still, he understood that most people were not like him and George Carlin.

Well, this was something. People had entered his apartment. It was a man he had never seen before, and Carol, who he did remember, and a very old woman he also had never met. This was strange. He lit another cigarette. And watched them come toward him. Unfortunately, he had not closed the window, so he could hear them.

As it turned out, the strange man claimed to be the owner of the building and Doughty listened to him from where he stood on the fire escape, as the man and the women stood stupidly in front of the window. The man tried to hand him papers but Doughty, of course, didn't move his arms to take them. The man then explained something about taping the papers on the door, and some other stuff. Doughty was bored and although he always controlled his emotions, inwardly he felt peeved. He had to admit to himself that this was a bit much. There was also something about the women being witnesses. The older woman, not Carol, was crying. HAHA. He laughed internally.

"Where is my daughter's stuff?" The old woman had disappeared and then come back. "This is her furniture? Where are her—where is it all?" Then she wept so hard that he was just embarrassed for her. Carol put an arm around her.

"What did you do, Doughty?" Carol said. "What did you do to her?"

The old woman seemed as if she were going to fall, and Carol was holding her up. Then she craned her neck forward, lifting her distorted, deeply lined face, and screeched, "What did you do to my daughter?" Then she put her hands over her face—that was a good move, no one wanted to see her face—and wailed. Carol held on to her, and was clucking like a hen.

From this, he surmised it was Sophia's mother. He wanted to say "Your daughter hated you," but he knew that talking was beneath him. There on the fire escape, he of course had his wallet on him. He never understood men who took their wallets out of their pant pockets, unless they were going to sleep. That was the only exception. Through the open window, he passed Resnik's card to the man who pretended to own Doughty's loft. He had to give him some credit. He didn't seem emotional. Doughty respected that. It showed some self-control, unlike the women, who were gesturing with their hands, their faces all contorted and lots of mwamwa blabla.

"Call my lawyer," Doughty said. "I'll call 911 if you don't

leave. You're trespassing." This was an idle thought, calling 911, but they didn't know his phone wasn't working. It didn't matter. They left. He smoked three more cigarettes. Three was a good number. Then he climbed back into his home, and examined the door. They had removed the entire lock. There was just a circular hole where it had been.

He wondered, Did his mother still have his father's toolbox? Did Blake have a toolbox? Blake definitely had a toolbox. He knew there was a drawer in the kitchen with fixing stuff in it. He opened it and found duct tape. Then he went back to the door. He walked into the stairwell and looked at his door from the outside. He walked back inside. He used the bolt lock above the key lock. He could lock it from inside. That was enough for now. He'd figure it out. So much had happened. All of it was good, but he needed to digest it all. Prioritize his next moves according to their importance.

Chapter 25

Stanny actually came over as planned. Not that Doughty worried he wouldn't, it was just that it had been a while, and during his time in the city, he'd noticed that people from uptown often got disoriented downtown. This was understandable. At one point, he'd been that way himself. Doughty met him outside the building and they walked up the stairs.

"Wow, these are a lot of stairs," Stanny said.

"True. I'll put an elevator in soon. But it's good to be high up, as you know. It's always one thing at a time. My contractor is a busy man. I have so many things going on at once." Doughty pushed the door open.

"What happened to the lock?" Stanny said. He was dutifully carrying a bottle of vodka, as Doughty had instructed. Funny, he had grown to like vodka. He blamed Sophia. What Doughty really wanted was crack—it had been a while!—but he'd told Stanny to bring some coke and vodka.

"I'm replacing it," Doughty said. He knew there was some

impatience in his voice. He was ready to party! "Where's the rock?"

"The rock?"

"I mean the coke."

Stanny looked at him and then looked around. "Dude, it smells bad in here."

"My housekeeper is taking care of her sick mother and, as you know, I'm a softy, so. She'll be in tomorrow. Where's the coke?"

"Jesus, Doughty," Stanny said.

Stanny followed Doughty into the kitchen. Doughty had washed the glasses himself and was going to say something like "I washed the glasses for you, you dick," but then chose not to put him in his place quite yet. "Nice space, right?"

"It's very arty."

Doughty poured the drinks and saw Stanny looking around. His friend wasn't as impressed as he should be.

"What's the smell?"

"I told you." Now Doughty was a little angry. Stan the Man was being rude. Also, he needed coke. "My cleaning lady is not around. Stop being a fucking dick." This happened when he was at his wit's end, but he forgave himself, he had been forgiving himself a lot lately. What with all that was going on. "Let's go sit down and do rails."

In the living room, he watched Stanny cut two lines on the coffee table. He watched his friend look around, clearly impressed with the size of his place, as expected. Doughty also knew that even though it was fun to dabble in the downtown world, eventually it wouldn't be the right place for a Darien man. Doughty did the two lines, his dollar bill already rolled up, and Stanny had an opinion about that.

"Dude, one for each of us, man," Stanny said.

"Fuck you, Stanny. You're in my house. And it's fun, right? Cool, yeah? But I do plan on selling it and moving uptown, of course." It was good coke. He had a glass pipe next to his bed so he went and retrieved it. It wasn't the same as smoking a rock, but he could stoop to freebasing occasionally.

"Stan the Man, have you ever freebased?" He had brought the bottle of vodka, too, and refilled their glasses. Doughty had always prided himself on being a good host. He knew he didn't need to be, he knew no one deserved anything from him, but sometimes, he tried to set a good example of how *they* should be to him.

Stanny got up. "What the fuck."

"There's a first time for everything, Stan." Then he had a thought. "Remember your first blow job? That was because of me."

Stanny sat back down and ran his fingers through his hair. "I don't know, Doughty. This is other level for me."

Other level. This was true. He was on another level from other humans. It was like there were humans, and then there was him. It was so clear. There were levels, levels as clear as his loft being on one floor and other lofts being on the floors below him. Were people living in those lofts? Yes. Did he even remember what they looked like? No. Why? Because he was on another level. It was that solid and real.

"Watch me," Doughty said. And Stanny did. Ever since they'd met each other, he had led the way. He was a leader and the responsibility was a big one, but he'd always been big enough to take that on. He was what was known as a "born leader."

After the coke was all smoked up, Doughty felt amazing, and Stanny had taken a little puff, too, but Doughty had given his friend a hard look. He knew Stanny was being educated pretty intensely now. It wasn't easy for his friend to learn a new thing. "I'm going to crack this open," he said, and lifted the pipe up.

"What?"

"We're gonna crack this open and scrape it."

Stanny had the same look on his face that he'd had when Doughty first lit the pipe.

"Dude, I'm leaving. Wow. I don't feel so great."

This made Doughty laugh. "Okay, man. I'll leave with you."

"I don't want you to come with me."

But instead of leaving, Stanny got up and ran to the bathroom. This was a sign he was about to shit himself. Sometimes, this happened with coke. He had to hand it to Stan. It was good coke. Maybe there was some laxative in it, but coke did that, made you shit.

AS THEY WERE leaving, Stanny rushing down the stairs ahead of him, Doughty said, "I have a surprise for you."

Stanny looked a bit sick. What a pussy, he thought. But it was nice to see his old friend.

"I think I've had enough surprises," Stanny said. "I want to go back uptown."

"Let's go get one drink at this bar a few blocks from here. I have a surprise for you there. Just a drink. I promise it'll be fun."

As they entered Milady's, with no Joe to stop them, Doughty just had that intuition, that sixth sense, and damn he was a genius—Beata was behind the bar. But once they got inside and settled on some stools, he did notice gross, red-faced, toothless Joe sitting at the end of the bar, where he always sat, smoking. He was irritated with Joe, but he decided to be the bigger man and he waved and said, "Hey, Joe." Then he looked at Stanny. Stanny looked a little stunned.

"I know everyone here," Doughty said to Stanny, then he gave him a big pat on his back. He felt like getting really drunk. "Beata! Your old friend Stanny is here."

She had her back turned to them. She was at the register. Upon entering, Doughty had seen her see them, so this back-turned-toward-them thing wasn't working. "Bring us two vodkas!"

"I don't think I want to be here, Doughty." Stanny stood. Then he whispered, "That's the Watertown girl."

"Yeah, man! She still has the same mouth!" Okay, maybe he'd said this a little loudly. He turned his excitement down a notch. "It's a high school reunion!" He knew it didn't make perfect sense. He was riffing, he was improvising. He knew Carlin did that during stand-up. Why not him?

Doughty put a hand on his friend. A heavy hand. Sort of a push downward. He didn't want to, but it was a moment where it was warranted. "Sit."

"Jesus," Stanny said, but he sat, rubbing his arm. "Calm down."

Beata came over, empty-handed. She looked over at Joe, then looked back at them. "Get out of my bar."

"Actually, this isn't your bar. I'm thinking of buying it. I've been buying property in the neighborhood." She wasn't moving and he wondered if she was trying to imitate his solid-rock ability. "Just get us a round."

When she brought them two shitty pours, he downed his glass and pushed it back to her. "I'll take another."

She went and got him another. In fact, she brought him a water glass full of ice and vodka. Now that was a drink. He almost laughed. Whatever.

"I haven't seen you in ages! I've been busy, so I apologize."

He drank. She stood with her bird hands on her bird hips, her thin mouth shut tight. She had on too much eyeliner. You can take the girl out of Watertown, but you can't take Watertown out of the girl, he thought.

Stanny stood again. He hadn't even finished his first drink! Doughty grabbed his arm but Stanny pulled away and Doughty, feeling kind, let him go. He was out the door before saying goodbye. Here was a moment where Doughty let disappointment wash over him. He knew that there was very little payback for kindness, for generosity, but sometimes, people did disappoint him with their lack of gratitude. He shook it off. Stanny was a pussy. This was nothing new.

He lit a cigarette and boom, there was Joe, next to him. "Hey, man," Doughty said. This was good. It was good to see Joe being friendly. Sometimes, people forgot their place in the world and then, for no reason whatsoever, they remembered it and behaved accordingly. "Good to see you, Joe. Want a drink?"

"Want some crack?" Joe said.

This was—forward. Again, Joe was just showing his roots. His unfortunate upbringing. No one discussed drugs openly at a bar. It was done outside a bar, or near where the toilets were, or inside a bathroom. Of course Doughty wanted crack. Who didn't want crack?

"Excuse us," Doughty said to Beata. She was still standing there, her hands on her tiny hips. She was definitely imitating him, his rock-solidness, although he never put his hands on his hips. He wanted to say something to her, but business first.

OUTSIDE, JOE OPENED the door to his van for him, and Doughty appreciated his manners. Interestingly, Joe chose to paint his van white, and he kept the outside of it immaculately clean, which was no small feat in the city. Inside was another matter, but understandable. It was like the inside was his cave, there were cigarette butts in the ashtray, an empty beer can on the floor. It smelled a little stale, weirdly reminding him of the den where he and his mother had watched *Wheel of Fortune*. Doughty got in and then Joe walked around and got in the driver's seat.

"In the glove compartment," Joe said, and Doughty found a packet containing four rocks and a pipe. Wow! He smoked.

Then Joe started the van and began to drive. Okay! Road trip! Joe drove so well.

"You're a great driver, Joe." He had killed a rock and he felt great. He rolled down the window and a breeze hit his face and it felt so amazing. It felt as if God were touching him. It felt perfect. Joe wasn't a bad guy after all. He was a good guy.

Sure, he was ugly. But ugly poor people had their purpose in this world. Joe had a purpose. He was good at driving! And he had rocks in his glove compartment! Then, as usual, a brilliant thought came to Doughty's mind.

"Joe, do you want to be my driver?"

"What?" Joe had turned onto the Brooklyn Bridge. They were driving toward Brooklyn but Doughty could turn his head and see the Manhattan skyline, lit up gorgeously against the night sky. There was no traffic and soon they were across the bridge and he thought of his storage unit.

"As I expand my business, I'll need a personal driver. I'll need a few drivers but you could be my personal driver." He couldn't help it. There was a stream of generosity pouring out of him. He loved helping people. He was always helping people. He was lit up with love. "Can you take me to my storage unit? I have one here in Brooklyn. It's like you read my mind!"

Joe was pulling over. There was a stunning view of Manhattan. It was a great, quiet spot on the East River, which stretched out before them, black and calm. Behind them were the empty warehouses of DUMBO, which stood for Down Under the Manhattan Bridge Overpass.

"Mind if I do?" Doughty said, and put another rock in the pipe.

"It's all for you, Dotty."

"It's 'Doughty.'" He had to do it. Joe deserved some education. Joe had gotten out and walked around the car and was standing next to Doughty's door. "You know behind us is the neighborhood called 'DUMBO.' It stands for 'Down

Under the Manhattan Bridge Overpass.'" Doughty looked out at the view of Manhattan. Amazing. He was both peaceful and enlivened beyond anything. "I like teaching people things."

Doughty stayed seated and smoked. Everything was the best thing in the world, but mostly his brain and his future were the best things. He liked how patient Joe was, standing there. Then Joe opened the door and this, too, inspired Doughty. Everything was so inspiring. "You know what, Joe?"

"No, Dotty, tell me what."

Doughty put the pipe down on the dashboard. "You could be a doorman for me, too. I'm not sure what place—the bar, where you practice, I'll probably buy that bar soon. I've seen you practice, or at my first building. I just bought a building on Mercer Street."

Doughty decided to step out. He stretched, taking it all in. The air was fine, and even fresh. He instinctively pushed his chest out. He could breathe like an Olympian runner. He was standing on a paved circle, not quite a parking lot, as theirs was the only vehicle there and there were no ordered spaces, no yellow lines, just the glitter of black cement, the soft kind, cushiony under his feet, surrounded by calm water. He decided to share some of his life with Joe. "I used to live in Brooklyn. Very briefly. I hate Brooklyn, but this is an interesting spot. Only because you can see Manhattan. In fact, I used to not like SoHo, but it's grown on me. I'm more of an uptown guy."

Doughty thought about the rocks left in the glove compartment. "Give me a second, Joe."

As Doughty reached into the car to get another rock, Joe grabbed his arm and Doughty heard a crack.

"What the fuck?" His arm hung loosely at his side. Then Joe kicked him with some impressive force and he fell. Joe was a quick one. Okay, well, this wasn't what he'd expected but he got up and started to walk toward the empty warehouses, but he didn't get very far and he fell again. This time, despite one of his arms feeling loose, or something like loose, he used his arms to catch his fall. Weirdly, his face still hit the dirt. Sometimes, people got rough. It was like being on the playground. Men could be childish. He had to be the grown-up now. "I'm not going to hire you if you pull this shit. Think of your career, Joe."

Joe was standing over him and then backed off a bit. Joe was showing some common sense. That's right, back off, Joe.

From his position on the ground, Doughty could see up to the nakedness of Joe's stomach hanging out of the bottom of his T-shirt. Doughty would say something if Joe weren't pissing him off so much. He'd say, "Tuck your shirt into your pants, Joe." Instead, Doughty looked away, tired of helping him, and using his good arm, he pushed himself to a standing position so he could walk toward the buildings. He'd find a gypsy cab or something. Good thing he knew all about Brooklyn and gypsy cabs. It was like seven bucks back to SoHo. Or it had been seven bucks from the Cherry Tavern to Brooklyn. Close enough. It was incredible he remembered that, he thought happily as he walked away from the car. His memory was superb. Sublime all the time. Now he was rhyming!

Then, suddenly, he felt a force on his upper back, and he was on the ground again.

This was too much.

He struggled but succeeded, of course, to get up onto his knees and he could see inside the back of the van. When had Joe opened the back of the van? It didn't matter. He was curious, though, he had to admit. The light from the cab of the van was on, so Doughty could see that the back was mostly empty, with a few dead pigeons scattered around. Suddenly, he was hit hard on the back, and found himself face down on the ground. He turned his head to the side, spit out some dirt.

"Ha!" Doughty said. "You do kill pigeons! I thought Beata was making it up!"

Joe was standing on Doughty's right hand, moving back and forth on it. People! Didn't he have ambitions? He was digging himself a hole, poor toothless Joe. Doughty wrenched himself up. For a moment, he thought he'd left his hand on the ground, but when he got to his feet, he noticed his hand was still on his arm. It didn't look good, though. He was just entirely pissed now.

"Enough!" he yelled. Standing there, he noticed he was taller than Joe. He knew it was out of character, to raise his voice. But he remembered that this was what happened when you became successful. He'd heard about it, and now it was happening to him. You had to get angry and you occasionally would lose control and you had to raise your voice to the minions. "The plebes," they'd called them back in high school. They'd called the townies "townies," but the general public was the plebes. It was short for "plebeian," which during the Roman Empire meant "the working class," those who were not citizens, who were not members of the patrician, senatorial, or equestrian classes. Remembering that definition made him miss his encyclopedias. And to think they were so near. When this nonsense was over, Joe would drive him over there. He had his keys on him! As always, he wasn't the forgetful type. He couldn't be, what with all his responsibilities. With success came so much responsibility. And people resented your success. Joe put his hand on Doughty's head and pushed him to his knees.

"You want to suck my dick, Dotty?"

"It's 'Doughty.' Not 'Dotty.' I didn't want to have to correct you, Joe, but this is too much. You've mispronounced my name too many times now. I didn't want to embarrass you for not understanding."

"Do you want to suck my dick, DOWDEE? HAHAHA."

This was so tiresome. Too much, too much.

"No, Joe, I do not. I have a friend, Amanda. I'm happy to introduce you to her. She does it for a living! She's great." Doughty decided he needed to sit. He was exhausted. He was angry! Joe went away for a moment and he felt great relief. He was gathering himself.

Then Joe came back and lifted Doughty to his feet. Good! He needed to get walking.

"Let's see that dick of yours." Joe had the crack pipe. It was empty.

Doughty had a thought. "I get paid to show my dick to people occasionally. Since you gave me all that rock, I can show it to you."

"Come on. Let's see it. Your big dick."

Doughty thought about the crack. He really had smoked a lot, but he had smoked a lot before. He was strong.

"You want to hit that crack pipe again, before you show me your dick? Here you go, Dotty." Joe gave him the empty pipe, which Doughty took with his free, working hand.

"There are more rocks in the glove compartment, Joe."

"Smoke the pipe, Dotty."

It was empty. He put it to his mouth and then Joe had the good sense to light it for him. Sucking hard, he got a mouth full of lighter fire.

"There's no crack left. Go get a rock from the van!" Doughty's throat was scorched and he threw the pipe on the ground and then Joe punched him in the mouth. First the fire, now this. His mouth was not happy. And now, he was on the ground again.

Then Joe kicked him in the mouth, right where he'd punched him. This was too much.

Doughty pushed himself up onto his knees. He held his lips firmly together. He was trying not to show his anger. Mr. Miyagi had taught him better than that. It was one of his many strengths, his ability to hide his emotions. He had the power. The power to contain his feelings. To leave others guessing what was going through his mind. His mind was his power and he had power over his mind. Some blood trickled out of his mouth, even though he had it closed. Weird. He felt it, the blood, itchy on his chin. His mouth was filling with liquid. He contemplated swallowing it. Otherwise, he was going to have to open his mouth. Maybe he should just open it for a second.

Doughty dropped his jaw, and blood poured out. For some reason, this made Joe laugh. He had a strange sense of humor, this Joe. Pretty much everything made him laugh. So, in fact, he didn't have a good sense of humor, not if he just laughed all the time at everything, like an idiot. Like the idiot he was.

"Stand up and show me your dick."

He did have a great dick. Doughty tried to stand, but he found that difficult. So he just stayed on his knees, that was fine for now. What he could do, to his great surprise, was unzip his pants with his working hand. He liked thinking on his feet, or in this case, even not on his feet. On his knees! He could improvise with all his skills.

His dick was limp. He had the urge to pull on it. He knew, even when limp, it was still an impressive dick. "You can suh ih ih u wan."

His mouth was leaking more blood. He didn't sound like himself. His shirt was a wet mess. It smelled like metal. Like burnt metal. Thank God he had the laundromat phone number on the wall of his loft. He had a brilliant thought! Amanda would do his laundry later.

"I can suh ih I wan!" Joe said. Then with the laughter. It was like a woman's cackle.

Joe didn't suck it, though, he just stood there. What else did he want Doughty's dick for? Good God. This was really too much. Doughty sighed, blood trickling down his chin. He tried to wipe it with his right hand, but it didn't move. Oh, right. His left hand moved.

"Suck it, Dotty. You suck it like Beata sucked it. Like you made her suck your friends' dicks. Come on! Come on, Dotty. I want to see you suck your own dick."

Doughty was tired of talking. He was tired of trying to

teach this oaf how to pronounce his name. He just shook his head. It was a dumb request. He couldn't suck his own dick, he'd tried it in high school and it was impossible. He rested his head on his chest.

"Aw, don't give up. Come on, Dotty." Then Joe went behind him. Doughty tried turning around to look at what Joe was doing, then his head was pushed down and it veered to the side and hit the dirt. He tried to push himself back up to a sitting position. Left hand, he thought. Just too much. He really was done with this nonsense.

"Oh, look, you missed. My bad," said Joe.

Doughty felt Joe, still behind him, grab his head by his hair and pull him up. Well that was something. At least now he was doing the right thing and helping him back up onto his knees.

Then Doughty felt something on his back. It came fast, a hard, unbelievably heavy weight. He heard an incredibly loud crack, like a massive ice break on a pond.

His face was on his dick! This was fascinating. He was in better shape, more flexible, than he'd been in high school! Of course he was. He was always improving, as a person. Always reaching new and higher levels. The strange thing was he couldn't move his face up and down or anything. He even tried moving his head to the left or to the right, but it just hung there.

"Come on, man. You got this. Come on. Suck your dick."

Doughty seemed to be transforming. His limberness. A jolt of euphoria surged through him, like a huge hit off the crack pipe. He got his dick in his mouth. Or he thought he did. Whatever was coursing through his almighty blood was amazing and it was as if he could do anything, which he had always known and which was why he was who he was. He could do anything. It was working. Ha! Maybe Joe wasn't that dumb.

Then he fell over onto his side. He tried to move his legs even though he couldn't feel them, but he saw them. They were there, at a strange angle but there. Was this what yoga was? Amanda once had said something about yoga. He was about to ask Joe something and then he forgot. He was going to ask him . . . Oh, he forgot again. He heard Joe walk away. But then he came back.

Doughty had mixed feelings again. He preferred not to have to think mixed feelings. It was always better to land on something straight away.

Now he really wanted to ask Joe something. Doughty started to say "Hey, Joe." Those exact words did not come out, but Joe stood next to where Doughty lay, and he leaned down toward Doughty's face, smiling his toothless smile at him.

"You saying something, Dotty?" Joe had the crack pipe in his hand. He shoved it deep into Doughty's mouth, down his throat.

Despite his frustration, Doughty lifted his head and something strange came out. It wasn't what he wanted to say. He was having some trouble. He just would keep trying. Nothing was useless. Sometimes, he had to work harder at things than he wanted to, despite his general knowledge and his ability to make highly efficient use of his own inner resources. Maybe he was making sense but he just, for whatever reason, didn't understand himself. That seemed possible. Some really smart and interesting words were flowing out of him, and it was not important that he understand them now.

Joe understood, or not Joe, the universe.

The universe had a perfect understanding of everything he was communicating, all the strange sounds coming out of him.

Joe leaned toward him.

"You know who is going to miss you, Dotty?"

What kind of question was that? Doughty saw two Joes now. He realized he liked Joe. He liked both Joes and he liked that Joe had made himself into two Joes.

Joe *was* funny. It was a good revelation. Even if things were coming to him a bit later than he wanted, Doughty always figured things out in the end. It wasn't "The truth will set you free." The truth was often a trap. Control was what set you free.

But sometimes truth led to control, and now that he knew the truth about Joe, that he *was* funny, he had a better grasp on, better control of, the situation.

"Who's gonna miss you, hey, Dotty?"

Then Joe lifted a brick—when had he gotten that?—and brought it down on his head. Doughty started laughing. But it sounded funny. Joe was being funny, he himself sounded funny trying to laugh. This thought made him laugh more, but it still didn't sound like a laugh.

"NOBODY, Dotty. NOBODY."

Then he saw the two Joes' faces in his face. Joe's eyeballs were so bloodshot all the time and his shiny blue eyeballs, all four of them, were mashing against his own eyes. Joe needed Visine. Doughty tried to let him know it—he had to get some Visine. But Doughty was choking a little, so he tried to stop that choking. He focused. It was the pipe, he knew. He just had to figure it out. He needed a moment.

From where he was lying down, his face turned to the left, the right side of his head on the dirt, which felt fine, a little gravelly, of course. He tried to lift his head, maybe look around more, but found himself unable to do so. Even if he couldn't move his head, he saw Joe walk to the van and shut the back door, then go into the van. He heard the engine start. He would begin by asking Joe where he was going. He thought, What would Mr. Miyagi do? He thought of the one power that had helped him get so far in life. Of course! He was a stone. An ancient stone. He summoned that energy and became a stone. He was going to transform from a rock of immobility to . . . He forgot. It was perhaps time for him to also go into his deep, transformative sleep. All the transforming was happening. Then, he'd get back onto his feet, after a great Doughty-strength sleep, and think on his feet. But not now.

A rock, a rock. No one could touch him now. No one could move him. He was unbreakable. He was the center of the earth.

Acknowledgments

Thanks to Mark Doten and Bronwen Hruska for your support of my work for over a decade now. I am so proud to be doing my fourth book with you. Thanks to Dr. Friedman, my partner in my fight for mental health and my guide in the examined life. My other therapists from the darkest time, Allison, Johanna, and Jo, thank you, too. Thank you to my early readers—Shya Scanlon, Sam Lipsyte, Julian Tepper, Thelma Adams, and Michael Pollock.

Shya, you especially read so many drafts and early essays and so on throughout my lengthy time of trying to figure out how to write what I needed to write. You were not only an early reader, but a life coach of a friend, a hugely patient friend.

Jack, this one is for Hal, but the next one is for you.

Thanks to my BGH community, to the bartenders and the regulars—Jill, Dylan, Arion, Malena, Rob and Donna, PJ, Mike, and anyone else I might be forgetting. Thanks to Zach and Stephen for your support not only at BGH but at my home.

Thank you to Jon Allen for loving me, making time for me, and believing in me for almost three decades.

I wrote and revised this novel at home and at various places, but mostly in Beacon at Graham's place and Jess's home for one amazing week, and at Birgit's in Las Terrenas. Thank you for giving me such great spaces to focus completely on the work.

And Susie Supercharged. If you had only been able to take me away when you asked to.

Friend family indeed. Community. And sons. Such amazing sons.